Marie Hess

BENEATH THE WILLOWS

BookLand press

Published by
BookLand Press Inc.
15 Allstate Parkway
Suite 600
Markham, Ontario L3R 5B4
www.booklandpress.com

Printed in Canada

Front cover image by Lario Tus

Library and Archives Canada Cataloguing in Publication

Title: Beneath the willows / Marie Hess.
Names: Hess, Marie, author.
Identifiers: Canadiana (print) 20220223661 | Canadiana (ebook) 20220223688 | ISBN 9781772311679 (softcover) | ISBN 9781772311686 (EPUB)
Classification: LCC PS8615.E785 B43 2922 | DDC C813/.6—dc23

We acknowledge the support of the Government of Canada through the Canada Book Fund and the support of the Ontario Arts Council, an agency of the Government of Ontario. We also acknowledge the support of the Canada Council for the Arts.

BENEATH THE WILLOWS

Table of Contents

Part Two

Part One

Beth had just finished making the bed when she noticed a robin landing on a branch just outside her window. She smiled for a moment as she sat on the edge of the bed.

"I've seen you before," she whispered.

In that instant her mind pulled her back to her childhood. Her family was sharecroppers and lived on an apple farm in Alcott, New York. They lived there for a number of years and eventually became sharecroppers on a tobacco farm. After years of plowing fields and hanging tobacco, her father had an opportunity to own his own farm in southern Ontario. It now seems so long ago. It was here Beth did an unexpected thing. She grabbed a notebook and pencil from the drawer next to the bed and began to write.

The year was 1948. At first sight of this old house, I wondered why my father would make such a deal without seeing it first. Some of the windows needed new glass. The front door stood leaning against the outside wall while the hinges and screws were nowhere in sight. Taking an old wooden ladder that was lying on the front porch, my father climbed to the roof.

"It will need new shingles," he shouted. "I will patch up the roof for now. Hopefully it will last till next spring."

My father reassured my mother and I that it would take a lot of hard work but it was fixable. And it wasn't long after, that I excitedly called out to my mother to hurry to the other side of the house where I sighted a swing hanging from the branch of an old maple tree. My mother had the biggest smile on her face as she also found an old shed that could be used to raise chickens.

Hearing the eagerness in my father's voice, we rushed to the back of the house. There stood an orchard full of red apples. We all smiled knowing mother's canned applesauce would be a real treat in the winter. My parents were true farmers saving and storing whatever they could for winter.

But that first winter mice had gotten into some of the food and had eaten a good portion of the seeds my father thought he had carefully stored. He blamed all the mice on the harsh winter we were having. It seemed like one storm would end and another would begin. There was nothing we could do but stay indoors and listen to the north wind howl.

While I sat at the kitchen window one blustery morning, I found myself in a dreamlike world, as children often do. The frost had magically sketched ice ferns all along the windowpane. And through this glass, I watched as winter displayed its beauty. The wind blew so strong that it lifted the snow from behind our house. It danced and swirled as it drew the snow upward, only to circle down again, as it pushed the snow between the tall evergreens. It continued its path, but in a blink of an eye it changed course. By the end of the day the drift was so high the old shed had disappeared.

Suddenly a cold breeze rushed into the room. I pulled my sweater tightly around me. And I watched as my father carried in an armful of wood and placed it next to the wood stove. My mother looked up and smiled while she continued to roll out the dough on the floured pastry board. The feeling of warmth and the closeness I felt at that moment instilled a memory of that day that would last forever. We didn't have much that first winter, but we survived.

My mother was right the birds would tell when it was spring. I woke that morning to the sounds of the birds singing in the maple tree just outside my window. While I lay in bed that morning, I could hear my parents making plans for the new crop, and how we would all have to work extra hard this year. Hopefully, we would have a good crop with maybe enough to take into the market to trade or sell for flour, sugar, and salt, things she would need in the winter for baking.

When the planting day arrived, we were up before the morning sun. It felt as exciting as a celebration. Some of our neighbours had already arrived pitching in wherever they could. Their spirits were high as they were joking and laughing. My mother joined in as she carried out the morning coffee. I promptly followed her out the door anticipating that I might be able to help or at least ride on the wagon.

My father turned giving me a stern look reminding me it was no place for children. He often told stories along with the other neighbours of how they all knew or heard of some child being backed over, or who lost a hand in the machinery.

When the last bag of seed (which would be hand planted) was heaved onto the wagon, my father again turned reminding me to fill the wood box.

"The womenfolk," my father said "will be busy cooking and baking. The men will be awful hungry when they return," my father said as he put on his hat and left for the field.

My mother never complained about cooking, it was her way of pitching in.

While filling my wagon as high as I could with firewood one morning, I thought I saw something out of the corner of my eye moving in the woods. I quickly ran to the fence line, only catching a glimpse of the tail end of a rabbit. I sat hidden among the high weeds while I waited for the rabbit to reemerge. It was here I felt strangely drawn into this forbidden place. It was in those lingering moments I felt its stillness, an unknown time of a forgotten world unfolded in my mind. A time when the word "Indians" (as they were called back then) gave a chill up your back. I let my imagination run as hideous faces headed into battle. For a long moment I could only see what I had created with my imagination. Who were these savage people that I only saw in books. An unnerving feeling ran through me as a sudden gust of wind circled the trees creating that rustling sound that I was now hearing. I could almost see them crouching, waiting to attack, but it was only in the mind of a child.

Released from my thoughts I could hear the stern voice of my father calling from a distance, scolding me for being so close to the forest. Still I couldn't let it go, what had happened that people were so afraid. For an endless time I sat on the back porch watching for any kind of movement within the forest while unanswered questions filled my mind.

My thoughts drifted back to when we first moved here. Mr. Woodberry, who lived about half mile away, stood knocking at our front door early one morning along with his wife Joan and their two children.

"You must be Nelson and Cora Wright," Mr. Woodberry said.

My father greeted them in while my mother made a fresh pot of tea, which went so well with Mrs. Woodberry's pies. They warned us that anyone who entered the forest, including any animals, never returned. Native land. Some say there's a whole Native community living within this forest, while others believe there are only a few still roaming through the woods. We all thought it odd that something like this was possible - a Sacred Forest - but my parents respected what he had said and our families quickly became good friends that year.

It was Mr. Woodberry who saw we didn't have a tractor that day and offered the use of his for when plowing season began. My father took him up on his offer. It was like a code the farmers stood by all over the county. They helped one another whenever there was a need. My father hoped that it would never change. It made for a strong community.

Looking back at those early years, I can almost feel the heat as my memories pull me back once again to the stillness of that first summer. That day the sun seemed to draw up what little moisture there was in the garden. My hot tired feet shuffled along from one plant to the next while I tried to keep up. It wasn't long before my mother suggested I get out of the sun. I had no sooner sat down next to our picnic basket, than she called out again.

"We'll be stopping for lunch soon. Careful you don't spill the water!"

Cautiously I poured a drink from the oversized pickle jar. The drinking water always seemed to be cooler in a tin cup. Leaning back against the trunk of the tree I quickly rid myself of my shoes. I smiled just a little as I watched the sand pour out of them. My imagination took me to a place where the piles of sand became hills, and small sticks became people. I amused myself till my parents arrived.

The weeds that year seemed to grow faster than we could pull them out. My father thoughtfully reminded us the land hadn't been plowed for a number of years. He would turn over the soil again late in the fall, killing most of the weeds before winter and that would give us a better start for next year's planting.

Although my parent's work never seemed to end until the sun went down, they never seemed to tire. It was the joy of seeing new plants sprouting up through the soil that would outweigh their labour. When harvest arrived we gathered the corn and beans for drying, while the potatoes and carrots were carried into the cellar for storage. In that moment a smile spread across my mother's face as she tightened the last lid on a jar of tomatoes. She turns just in time to see my father walk through the doorway.

Taking a handkerchief from his pocket, my father slowly wiped the dirt and sweat from his face while he told my mother his concern. It was the look on his face that told me there wouldn't be enough for all of the winter.

"The neighbours are saying there hasn't been many deer come through this area for a long time. I guess we'll just have to settle for rabbit this winter," my father said with a smile as he tried to make light of the situation.

There had to be plenty of deer and rabbits in the woods just behind our property, I thought. I was confident that I could set the rabbit traps as my father had taught me. I wouldn't go directly into the forest and I would only stay just inside the fence line, I told myself.

The Sacred Forest

From a distance there wasn't anything different or unusual about this forest, but as you came closer you could see the forest was thick with undergrowth making it almost impossible to see inside. And everyone said, without a doubt, they felt they were being watched. Of course, there were stories that were told about animals or pets entering and never returning, and occasionally we would hear stories of teenage boys boasting they had entered and returned without a scratch. But none could say who it was or what family they came from. Nevertheless, people were afraid.

All we knew were Native people lived in this forest and it had some kind of protection placed on it some hundreds of years ago.

The next morning, I got up extra early and went to the edge of the woods. With the snares that I previously found just inside the barn, I stepped into the woods. It didn't feel any different. I quickly looked around finding a familiar looking path. Rabbit trails, they were everywhere. Before I knew it, I was covering the last trap with leaves. When I stood up, I couldn't believe my eyes. My home was nowhere in sight.

No matter which way I turned, the trees looked unfamiliar. With no markings to go by, I was lost. I wanted to scream, shout, anything to get my parents attention. I held my hands over my mouth in fear of what lived here. My tears flowed uncontrollably as father's voice kept going through my mind.

"If you ever get lost, stay where you are. I'll find you."

He didn't know this forest. No one did. I was lost! I knew then I would have to find my own way out.

It didn't seem like I walked very far, but I grew tired, or was it the monotony. Every tree looked the same. There was no time here, no sunlight to go by. Only the rustle of leaves my footsteps made broke the silence, as the forest grew unnervingly still. It was here that I stumbled and at that same moment I heard the sounds of snapping twigs.

Something was rushing through the woods. I didn't wait to see what it was. I just ran as fast as I could in the opposite direction, unaware darkness was just ahead of me. I was running blind with no thought of what was in front of me. Feeling the sting on my face, my arms seemed to develop a will of their own as they thrashed the branches and thorn bushes from my face. I had to keep running. I could feel it almost on me.

Suddenly, I felt my ankle twist as it reached out grabbing my foot sending me to the ground. I didn't know how long I lay there. But when I woke, I could feel its tight grip as I struggled to be free. Frantically, I reached out searching the darkness for any kind of stick or rock to defend myself. At that moment I could feel it loosen its grip. I immediately fell back against the ground while my heart raced in my chest.

The night was still now. Whatever it was, it had vanished in the darkness, but for how long? I knew I had to keep moving, but it was the dim light in the distance that caught my attention. I hastily made my way through the bushes. To my amazement, there stood a cabin.

Crouching down low, I cautiously looked into the small window. Only a small light stood flickering against the stillness of this darkened room. I stepped inside knowing I should not have. But anything was better than staying outside with that thing running around. Cautiously, I crossed the dimly lit room wondering who lived here. As I reached for the latch to an adjoining room I cautiously whispered, "Can you help me, I'm lost." There was never an answer.

There stood the most inviting sight - a huge bed. Fur covered its bulkiness while straw burst out from the sides. I closed the door behind me, falling asleep immediately without a thought of who lived there. When I awoke the next morning, I felt the warmth of the morning sun as it fell against my skin. I had such a restful sleep and was about to stretch and yawn when I heard something moving in the next room. I froze in place as my heart began to race as I anticipated the worst. I shook my head in disappointment knowing I shouldn't have come into someone's home.

Through a crack in the door, I could see a man. He stood six feet tall. His shoulders were broad while his long dark hair reached the length of his back. With his large appearance, he seemed awkward stooping over a wood stove, gently stirring in a pot. I soon realized that I was not going anywhere. The only window in the room was too small to escape from. Again, I held my eye to the crack of the door. This time his eyes met mine, my legs buckled beneath me.

When I awoke, he was kneeling beside me asking, "Satakari:te ken?" (Are you well) helping me to stand he led me to a kitchen table, which I was sure he cut from the base of a large oak tree.

"Satonkariaks ken?" (Are you hungry) "Saniata-thens ken?" (Are you thirsty) he said as he held up a dipper of water.

"Yes," I said as I shook my head.

"My name is Isaac. I've made you something to eat. But first, I'll put something on that cut of yours," he said.

I never asked how he had learned the English language, but I was happy he did.

"My name is Beth Wright."

My words were almost in a whisper. My head instinctively pulled back as if part of me were being seized. I didn't much like giving my name to a stranger. I watched his face for any kind of uncertainty on his part, his face was gentle. I quickly spoke up when I caught him glance back at me.

"I must have fallen pretty hard out there in the woods," I said as I felt the side of my head.

Isaac nodded his head in agreement as he stepped outside, returning a few minutes later with a large leaf he'd picked from the ground.

"It will help heal your wound," he said.

"Last night I could hear twigs snapping, and the sound of heavy footsteps like someone running real fast coming through the woods. I was about to see what was out there, when I noticed you going in the direction of my home. You had fallen asleep on my bed by the time I got into the house, so I let you sleep," Isaac said.

I quickly apologized for going into his home. "But something was in the woods chasing me. When I saw the bed I only intended to rest. I've never slept on a straw bed before," I said.

"Onó:ra" (corn husks), he corrected. "They're 'onó:ra kentskareh (cornhusk mats). You stack enough on, they make for a good sleep."

I had no fear of this man, yet I had just met him. He spoke in such a slow, calm manner I felt that I could listen to him forever.

"I've lived in the forest all of my life and have never seen anyone as young as you come this far into the woods," Isaac said while he gently pushed a bowl in front of me suggesting I eat. His large hands implied he was somewhat stronger than my father, yet there was gentleness about him.

I told him my family was new to the area, and how we had struggled this last year.

"We are vegetable farmers," I said proudly. "I entered the forest just to do some trapping to help put food on the table," I said in my innocence.

His people also cultivated the land. He didn't know how many of his people were left, but his ancestors they had settled here more than two hundred years ago. When I asked about the forest and why he lived here alone, Isaac raised his head and made a gesture to follow him outside.

I quickly followed to where he sat down in front of an oversized log that looked to be burned only in the center. He then began to tell an extraordinary story his maternal grandmother Sarah once told him.

A Story of Long Ago

"It was long ago," Isaac began as he picked up a stone chisel and proceeded to clean away the charred remains of a burned out stump.

"I can remember that day so clearly. I was just a small child at the time. Akhsótha (My grandmother) and I had settled along the river. The air was still that morning as my Akhsótha Sarah sat weaving her basket, and it wasn't long before she began to take me back into her past.

Tears soon filled her eyes as she recalled the hardships they had gone through to get to this land. An Indian agent had come to her village having earned the trust and respect of our people. He spoke of tsi nahoten ne akwekon onhwentsya wa'onkhirharatsten ne onkwehonwe land (that was promised for our people), a land of abundance.

One family had resisted, a man name Wolf. He felt uneasy about leaving, along with his two brothers and their families. He argued. It was foolish to leave when there is plenty right here.

Wolf was my great rakhsotha konha (grandpa) and Sarah was his only daughter of nine children," Isaac said. "Sarah was named after the Indian agent's wife. Her mother had become good friends with her after the woman had given her a set of English tea cups, and the name Sarah sounded real nice when you said it.

The name Wolf was given to him when he was just a young man because of the manner in which he could track. It was said that he could crawl along in the woods and go through underbrush without breaking a single twig. He could track the deer so well that he would be sent out alone, circling around sending them in the direction of the other hunters at the edge of the woods.

Our people only killed what they could eat, never any more. The hide was cleaned before being stretched between two trees. It was used for their footwear and clothing. And when the day was done, my people always gave thanks to the Creator for the things they had taken from the earth."

I was fascinated listening to the past and eager to hear more.

"Months had passed and after lengthy talks, it was decided. Our people would start preparing for the long journey, gathering whatever they could carry. Special care was given to the children and the elders.

With the promise of land that was set aside for our people. A land that was plentiful and a river that was as blue as the sky flowed between the lands, which would take them wherever they wanted to settle. Our people set out with strong hearts and minds.

Wolf, his brothers, and their families said their farewell and wished their people a safe journey. The weeks passed on and Wolf soon realized with more settlers moving in, they would have to follow the trail their Chief had taken. Wolf reassured his daughter, Sarah, they would make it. They would hunt and fish along the way.

Sarah was a quiet child and mostly stayed by herself. She would spend most of her time studying plants.

The Elders would say just leave her alone. It was natural for her.

One day, as Sarah stood pounding dried corn in a hollowed out tree stump (to make their corn bread) her thoughts soon drifted elsewhere. She still didn't feel right about leaving, especially after she had noticed something odd in the garden a year earlier. All the plants had produced double. The beans, the squash, the ears of corn were fused together in twos on every plant. She didn't know how, but she knew that it meant that there would be a food shortage in the near future.

By the end of the week, her parents, along with her uncles and their families had packed all they could carry. Sarah sat one last time under her favourite tree. She always loved the way a huge root had sprouted up out of the ground making a perfect seat. Leaning back against the tree, she sat gazing up into the branches.

Her thoughts drifted back to a time when the woods seem to be full with her people. Winter was near its end and it was time to tap the sugar maples. She remembered how excited the children were as their parents prepared to set up a makeshift home in the woods. Upon their arrival, the children would eagerly rush from tree to tree while their parents inserted wooden taps into the trees. Containers made of birch bark sat at the base of the tree catching the sap. The sap was then gathered and carried to a larger pot and brought to a slow, steady boil.

Sarah recalled her parents taking turns through the nights, along with the others, to keep the fires burning. In the morning, they would wake to the sweet smell of wahta ohshehs (maple syrup). When it was thick enough, it would be stored and used in their favorite dishes. In the winter, as a treat, her mother would boil the syrup until it was thickened, then pour it into cones made of birch bark.

Wiping the tears from her face, Sarah looked out onto the small brook that weaved in and out between the trees. A blanket of wild flowers scattered the bank, enhancing the beauty that Sarah would always have etched in her mind. Sarah hung her head, her fingers tightly squeezing some of her favorite coloured stones, while she closely held her cornhusk doll near her. She imagined her faceless doll was sad as she sat looking out at a scene that could never be replaced, her home.

When called, Sarah took her place near her mother. She would not look back in fear her tears would hinder their spirits. They were also hopeful as they started their long journey to the new land. They couldn't have imagined the length of time it would take and the toll it would have on their bodies without proper food, water and rest.

One night after an exhausting day, they set up camp. It was a beautiful clear night as they lay beneath the star filled sky. An ever so slight breeze from the north flowed over their tired swollen feet while their minds slowly drifted off to better times. It helped to compensate for the aches they felt from the day. They dreamt that night, their bodies floating off to the land of good hunting and fishing. In the dream, they were standing looking over the riverbank as hundreds of fish swam in front of their feet. The forest animals were everywhere.

Waking to a new day, they gave thanks. With the dream instilled in their minds from the night before, it gave them the courage to travel on. Week after week, they followed the path of their people. Their once lively steps now turned to drudgery as they pushed their weary bodies to exhaustion each day through the unknown land. Day after day, the sun would beat down on them. With no release from the heat, water was becoming scarce.

They soon realized they had run into a drought, but by this time it was too late to turn back. With no water, Wolf and his brothers knew the animals were long gone at the first sign of a change in the land. Not even the plants for their medicine that grew near water could be found. Without enough food and water, they became weaker and weaker. The women and children couldn't walk any further.

Wolf set up camp while his brothers scouted ahead. They came back with heavy hearts. They had recognized the marking of a burial site. They were on the right path but something was happening to our people. That night they slept with empty stomachs.

The next morning, they woke to the unmistakable smell of tea that was made from leaves and stems of the juniper tree. The juniper tree is an excellent survival food for the berries and the bark are all edible. A large piece of meat hung over the fire. Wrapped inside the meat were wild onions and herbs, but where had these things come from, they questioned?

Sarah spoke of a man that came through the bushes in the night. He was from our tribe but she didn't recognize him. He had long black hair with a claw mark on the left side of his face. Sarah began to tell them an amazing thing about this man. When he walked, his feet never touched the ground. He stood at the foot of her mat as her family slept and gave Sarah a message to deliver to her father. They were to eat well, to gain their strength for they were needed up ahead.

Sarah's father never knew her as a storyteller, he would think on what she had said. Two nights had passed, still they didn't leave. Again the man with a scar on his face came to the camp. This time he held out his hand to Sarah, and she took it. As she looked back, she could see her family asleep on the ground. Sarah floated above the trees, and over the hills, to a place where she saw a brook of clear spring water, and strong healthy green trees and plants. The man described the plants she would need for their medicine. They continued on to where the land became dry with little vegetation. It was there that she saw her people in great desperation.

Turning away, she couldn't stop her tears. When she looked again, she was lying back on her mat. Sarah had to convince her family to leave, but how? There lying on the ground was an unusual feather, she picked it up and fastened it into her hair.

When she woke her father, she told him of the new message. Again her father questioned her. How was it no one else has seen this man? She didn't know, but each time he left she had found a feather lying on the ground. She showed her father how she had fastened them in her hair. Her father knew this rare feather and believed it must be a sign. He ordered Sarah to go quickly and wake everyone.

That day, they found all the food they needed and fresh water that was put in pouches and clay jars to be carried to their people. It was at this time that Sarah used all her knowledge of plants. She knew exactly where to find them and what plants were edible. She was to look for all the berries she could find especially the seedpods of the wild rose to prevent scurvy. When they had all that they could carry, they set out in the direction Sarah described. They walked all day and through the night.

When they arrived, they could hardly believe their eyes. Our people were barely alive as they lay on the ground. One man stood out above the rest. Sarah recognized him right away from the deep wound in his face, but when she turned to tell her father, he was nowhere in sight.

Sarah's father and the others scrambled to help their people although it was difficult to recognize them. They had lost so much weight. When Wolf asked where his friend was, they told a story of bravery, how his friend had fought to save their people from a wild dog attack and had died of his injuries.

Wolf remembered what his daughter had said and asked if his friend had any cuts on his face.

"A large wound on the left side of his face," their chief said.

He had been too weak to fight a good battle, but had managed to destroy the crazed animal. With his weakened condition, his body couldn't heal his injury. He was too weak to help any longer. However he found that he could in spirit and he knew Sara was the only one he could contact. They were glad Sara had trusted her instincts. She would keep her name, but she would always be known as a konwatya'tonhkwátkens (vision walker).

With their health improving each day, they prepared to travel on. When they arrived in the new land, game was plentiful. The forest was strong with a heavy growth of trees and plants. You could walk for days in the woods. It stretched for miles upon miles in any direction.

But when the Europeans O'serón:ni' (white people) arrived in this land, they continually cut the trees to clear land for their homes with no thought for our future. My people knew that once the forest was gone, this would affect the birds and the animals population. Our people couldn't stop what was happening to the trees or to the plants that were needed for our medicine. Venison, a main diet of our people, was becoming scarce. It was in those days we found many animals that were hunted and left lying dead on the ground. In just a short time, we would die of starvation.

It was a practice of our people to come together with our Elders in times like this. In one voice, it was decided that the forest had to be protected. They would perform a ceremony to protect this forest from being destroyed. After the ceremony, the animals and birds that entered were protected and could not leave until the forest was renewed and game was plentiful once more. Many of the original families that walked the journey from the Mohawk Valley still live here within the forest. Still, there are many like myself who chose to live away from the village, still keeping watch. Many of our Elders have passed on, along with my parents and my great-great grandmother Sarah who lived till she was a hundred and one. Her spirit continues to exist in this Sacred Forest to this day.

The Garden

When Isaac finished the story of his maternal grandmother, he immediately stood up. Not saying another word, he motioned for me to follow him while he carried the three-foot stump he was preparing.

A short distance away through the woods was another clearing. It was just as he described. My vision of Sara's past became real when I saw the hides being dried, stretched between two trees. Nearby was the remains of a tree stump "yowha:ronteh" (where there was a hollow in it), Isaac said while poining to where it had been chipped away. Its once smooth outer surface was now etched with coarse grooves weathered through time. Its basin still held traces of white corn while the kanenhstane'koń:reks (corn pounder) stood leaning against the wall just inside a makeshift shed.

"I've been meaning to replace it for some time," Isaac said with a slight grin.

It was the dried cornhusk rustling in the distance that next drew my attention. I hurried to see what he had grown. Large squash littered the garden along with piles of dry beans, as well as heaps of potatoes. A tree branch made a perfect hanging place to dry his corn. The onó:ra (corn husks) were pulled back exposing the white corn to the sun as cob after cob had been fed into a braid, until it resembled a large cluster of grapes. There was a lot my family could learn from his style of preserving. I smiled knowing our families were similar. He also was preparing for winter.

And while I stood looking out over his back garden, I felt a familiar feeling of comfort here. The trees were huge that surrounded his property. I started to see the forest not as just rows of trees, but as a power, a strength protecting all living things. And at that moment Isaac placed his hand on my shoulder and smiled. He seemed to know what I was thinking.

"I built my cabin long ago for my wife and myself, and planted most of the fruit trees along with a good number of the wildflowers you see here," Isaac said as we headed back to his cabin.

The place was beautifully kept. He had no children and his wife had passed on some years before. With the sun setting, Isaac suggested we should eat before it got too dark. When we sat down at the table he handed me a big bowl of what looked like kernels of white corn, but double in size. It was called onénhstohkwa (corn soup) and it was delicious.

Insisting that I take his room that night, I watched from the window as Isaac placed a large log on the campfire and rolled out a cornhusk mat. Not able to sleep, my thoughts of the day were racing through my mind. I decided to join my new friend and quickly made myself welcome on a log near the fire. The smell and the sound of the wood crackling in the fire instantly lured me back to a time shared with my parents not long after we moved here. We had worked all day cleaning the yard and picking up dead branches that fell the winter before. We lit a fire that evening and lay beneath the stars. I guess it almost seemed magical because we woke the next morning knowing in our minds the way the farm was going to be, right down to the plowed fields and rows of apple trees.

Again, I tried to apologize to Isaac for taking his bed.

"I've always preferred sleeping outdoors. I know every sound in this forest, although I'm puzzled that you made it in this far without me knowing," Isaac said.

Not of Native descent, how had I made it this far I questioned? Isaac seemed distant, lost in his thoughts, but then turned.

"You might try to get some sleep. In the morning I'll take you home," he said.

Waking at the break of dawn, I watched through the window as my friend gave thanks to the Creator for the new day. The hike home would be long, but I felt better knowing Isaac was just beside me. I told him about the strange animal that had chased me through the woods.

His mouth twisted into a slight grin. "Was it making a grunting, snorting sound?" he asked.

"Yes it was," I explained excitedly. "And it had grabbed my foot, pulling me to the ground," I said.

Isaac pointed to the ground about twenty feet away where leaves and dirt were thrown about. "Is this what grabbed your foot?" he questioned.

Isaac pointed out a large root sticking up out of the ground. "And that noise you heard. It was a pig. A stray from a farmer's field I guessed. I caged it up a few days ago, but it had gotten loose," Isaac said. We both laughed at the thought of being chased by a pig.

The sun was setting as we arrived at the edge of the woods. When I turned to say goodbye, Isaac was gone.

My family didn't know what to make of my story about being lost in the woods, or the fact that a kind man named Isaac had guided me home. But they were glad I was safe at home. The truth is they never said much about the Native land again. But every now and again in the late spring I could have sworn I've seen him in the midst of the trees. Strangely, I would find another leather pouch filled with seeds lying against the fence.

Going through my adolescent years, I saw less and less of my friend named Isaac. It wasn't till I sat near the edge of the woods one quiet afternoon that I realized we had grown into one of the biggest vegetable farms in our county. It was here that I realized my fondest memories would always be tucked away in a special place in my mind. The seasons seemed to pass by quickly after that time. My interests were changing. I guess I was growing up inside and maybe it was time to find my own place in the world.

It would be many years before I would return.

Returning Home

Sitting out on the back porch having my morning coffee, a feeling of peace and content filled my mind as I watched my sons playing in the morning sun. It had been a long time since I'd been back home. Arriving late the night before, the trailer still packed stood in the driveway.

After fifteen years of marriage, my husband and I had divorced. I decided I would leave the city and move back to the old homestead. It had been over eight years since my mother passed on. Three months later my father followed. I never realized how much I missed this old house, so many memories. The house was well kept.

The tenants who were left in charge of the upkeep of the farm had more than done their job. A visible inspection from my porch told me the surrounding area of land on either side of our farm was slowly being built up with homes. I could see in the very near future, the remaining land would be made into a residential area. A feeling of pride came over me as miles of trees stood strong as ever just behind our farm.

Eating a late breakfast that morning, the boys suddenly scrambled from their chairs returning a few seconds later with a calendar. Their eyes lit up with excitement.

"What are we going to do today?" they asked, reminding me that it was the first day of summer, the longest day of the year.

It would be something that didn't cost money, and it was something the family could do together. Baseball! It had become a tradition with our family, inviting whoever wanted to play from our neighbourhood, a game of softball or twenty-one.

I would call a few of our close neighbors. I was sure they would play or at least watch the game. I was just about to pick up the phone, when the boys again jumped up excitedly pointing out the window. There was some kind of digger at the edge of the forest, just off our property. They just couldn't sit still until they could see the bulldozer up close.

They had to be a new company that was hired. Everyone knows that no one can enter that forest, and if they did they wouldn't return. Making a short cut across the open field, I spotted two men at the edge of the woods. One was a heavy built man wearing a red checkered shirt, the other a small wiry man. His straight blonde hair kept falling just over his right eye.

"We've had nothing but problems since we started clearing this land," the heavier man shouted. "The bulldozer runs a few minutes and then just quits!"

"The same with the chainsaw," the thin man added as he pointed to the young maple he had cut. "But in the opposite area it is like a barrier. Nothing seems to work. The surrounding community seems to think that this land is sacred."

They left that day assuring us they would be back.

A few months had passed and my sons were settling in nicely. I had read in the local newspaper that a nine year old girl named Lisa was missing. Her friends last saw her at the edge of the woods when the doll that she was playing with suddenly flew over the fence. But this was not surprising to the other children, especially when little Collin Spencer was near. He was the only one in school that saw humor in everything he did. He just loved to laugh. Of course it was at everyone else's expense!

Her friends had warned her to stay away.

"Just leave the doll," they shouted as they pulled her away.

That didn't stop Lisa. After they walked her home, she went back to retrieve her favourite doll. I was just about to take a walk around the edge of the woods where the doll was thrown when I spotted Allen Waters coming up my driveway. Officer as he preferred to be called, he was a good kind-hearted man that everyone cared about and respected. He didn't seem to walk as tall as I remembered. Word was he had a bad accident a few years back in some kind of high-speed chase. He had left the main road in pursuit of his assailant taking the River Road, once an old Indian trail.

"You'd think, after all these years, they would have straightened this road out," he mumbled to himself. Allen hated this road - too many sharp bends. "It's only a matter of time before someone is going to lose his life on this road," he said.

That was the last thought he had until a week later. After taking the first bend in the road, he hit a fog patch smashing into the assailant's car, where it had been abandoned only minutes before, smack dead in the middle of the road, sending Allen Water's car end over end. He recovered, but always walked slightly stooped over.

The pain inflicted on his back with every step he took, was slowly becoming etched in his face. Everyone knew, without a doubt, he would stay on the job till his retirement. His job was his life. He had known my parents just like everyone else around here. Most were born and raised here.

When Allen stepped from his car, he immediately greeted me with a tip of his cap, a trait of his.

"You must have heard about the little girl," Allen began. "Well, I'm here to ask if you will help find her. I'm at my wits end," he said. Sweat was streaming down his face as he loosened his tie and top button. "I can't seem to find anyone willing to go into the woods with me," he said.

I reminded Allen that it had been a long time since I had been in the forest. Things had to have changed in there.

Allen's voice suddenly took an uneven tone as he leaned toward me whispering, "There have been a number of reports in the last month or so. Your neighbor, Mrs. Hickles, called and complained of seeing sometimes up to four Natives crouching down, just inside the forest, wearing nothing but a breechcloth. They appeared to be hunting, always just before sunset or dawn. Another of your neighbors, Joe Bentley, also spotted a strange fire just inside the forest while walking his dog. He rushed home to call our fire department. A dozen of our local men responded, but there was no fire."

Allen immediately pulled a handkerchief out of his pocket, and wiped his brow. He stood there awkwardly moving from one foot to the other, waiting for my answer. It seemed to me, I was the only one that could find her.

"I will go. Alone!" I said.

A sigh of relief escaped from Allen's mouth as his head nodded in agreement.

Finding a sitter for the boys was going to be the easy part, Anna Gale. She was one of my closest neighbors and a good friend of the family. She was the perfect sitter for the boys. An image of a perfect grandmother came to mind right down to the thin rimmed glasses and ruffled apron. When she opened the door, the aroma of freshly baked cookies filled the air.

"You're just in time for milk and cookies," she chuckled.

The boys quickly took a seat. I remembered I had sat at this very table many times. Her husband Joseph sat reading the paper dressed in his brown suit. He dressed each morning like he was going off to work. A habit he kept over the last ten years after his retirement. It didn't feel right not dressing up in the morning, he once said. Sometimes he would stand in front of the mirror remembering how his wife had looked at him, telling him how handsome he looked in his suit. After all these years, she never once stopped straightening his tie before he left the house. He missed walking along the main street in town slowly making his way past the community bank where he had spent so many years. And he really didn't mind the children in town calling out to him as they went off to school.

"What's the time Mr. Greentree?"

He'd pull out his pocket watch, shout back the time, and smile. It had been twelve years since the bank ran that ad showing Mr. Greentree on the front cover, sporting a new suit and holding a pocket watch he received for his achievement that year.

Returning to the Sacred Forest

Saying goodbye to my sons, I hurried home to pack the things I might need for the journey if by chance my old friend was not there. Throwing the knapsack over my shoulders, I climbed over the fence where I had crossed years ago. A chill ran though my body as I stepped onto the sacred land, stopping me in my tracks. Suddenly, I became aware of my breathing as I drew in a deep breath. I couldn't believe my eyes. The fence, my home was completely gone. It was now clear just how I lost my way years ago. The opening had always been here. Retracing my footsteps, I found I was on the outside looking in. I had found the gateway. Taking a quick look around to assure my secret, I stepped back into the forest tying my kerchief around a tree, securing my only way out.

The birds led the warning that I was there, as their voices sang out. Small animals scurried away under shrubs and low branches while two deer gracefully sprang into the air while a buck raised his head in the distance. His brown eyes seemed even darker as rays of sunlight shone through the tops of the trees just behind him, giving him the appearance of importance. The buck continued to keep a watchful eye while I went on my way.

The forest was full of green foliage. Nothing here had been disturbed. Only the scattering of dead branches lay beneath the once strong maples. Tender young trees sprouted up everywhere.

I tried to imagine what the little girl might be going through. After all, I had been here before. It was the uncertainty that would frighten her, not the forest. Or was I wrong? There was something different. I could feel it!

A sapling, its leaves crumbled, lay on the ground. I pictured in my mind the little girl standing here, wondering which way was home while she was unconsciously tearing at its leaves. Or maybe it was just a small animal. I had to follow my instinct.

The further I walked, the more the land seemed to incline. It was only when my footsteps grew heavy, that I realized the distance I had travelled. And all the while darkness had followed close behind. I struggled to find one more clue before the sun settled behind this mighty forest. And as I did, something odd caught my eye. In the distance, all the trees were now taking on different forms as shadows grew everywhere.

The forest was coming alive, changing right before my eyes. Shadowy figures appeared out of nowhere. Fear rushed through me as I panicked to find a way out of this inescapable darkness. Immediately, I spotted a thicket of small trees crossing over each other. Its cave like appearance beckoned me to follow. Without another thought I dove in head first, escaping into a dark tunnel made of branches and twigs. A damp musty (sour) smell lingered everywhere. The caged in feeling gave me a sense I was safe here. The darkness and hollow sound created a depth I couldn't imagine.

I quickly reached for my flashlight. My memory suddenly took me back to the fence line where I had eagerly sat my backpack down while I tied my kerchief to a tree.

This place had to be a beaver's tunnel, but larger. Whoever they were that stood amongst the trees, they weren't following. I huddled in silence as the minutes turned to hours. I realized then I had no choice other than to travel on through this damp, dark, winding burrow. Its jagged branches sprung up everywhere cutting into my knees and back. It was only when the sand started to trickle down that I realized they were just above me.

I froze in place. As my breathing became silent, my ears strained to pick up any sound of what might be in store for me. Hearing the sound of footsteps snapping under their weight had my heart racing. Still I crept along feeling my way through darkness as my mind fought against the vastness I might have to travel, but the further I went the louder the sounds became. It grew so intense I feared that at any moment they could reach in and pull me out. Then, without the slightest warning, there was silence. Slowly, I crept along feeling for any small branches that could snap under my weight and alert them to my whereabouts. It was here in the darkness I found a familiar shape wedged between the damp branches, was this shoe of the missing girl. What happened that the young girl had to leave her shoe behind?

My fears were quickly replaced with concern for the little girl. Could she have made it in this far to a fork in the tunnel? Did we both take the same path? I began questioning my thoughts.

I kept telling myself she might be just ahead, maybe somehow trapped, needing my help. I've heard of beaver tunnels reaching a hundred feet as it twists and turns. And when I do find the little girl, what if she is injured, how will I ever get her out? What if there is no way out? My thoughts were running rampant, as the darkness finally took control of my mind with inescapable doom.

Mentally drained, my mind fought desperately to block the images. I would be trapped here and never found.

Realizing my fate, the air suddenly became heavy as my throat tightened. Hysterically, I pounded my fist against the wall and with the last desperate move I kicked as hard as I could, fighting desperately for air. To my surprise, I stumbled forward, landing in a clearing. The fresh air seems almost sweet to my lungs as I drew in a deep breath. My mind was free, as a veil of desperation was lifted.

When I regained my footing, I couldn't believe what I saw next. Several Native warriors passed only a few feet in front of me. Their eyes filled with anger as they caught sight of me. These ghostly beings quickly rose up, encircling the trees only to swoop down inches from my face. But as suddenly as a fog appeared in the distance, they vanished. The fog continued to grow in size while it weaved in and out between the trees.

I stood motionless, unsure of what was about to take place as it edged itself in front of me. To my surprise, there stood a woman dressed in white buckskin. Her brilliance seemed to light up the forest around her. She stretched her arms out and I was immediately standing alone in front of the cabin, with the warmth of the morning sun against my back. It seemed so long ago that I stood in front of this door. Cautiously, I stepped inside, wondering if Isaac even lived here anymore.

It was the sun's rays that shone just over his bed from a nearby window that created haziness in the darkened room. My eyes strained to see what was in front of me. Standing over my friend was a man in full Native dress, his long grey hair reaching the end of his back - a medicine man. He appeared to be holding a clay jar as if to give my friend a drink. Roots and leaves lay about on a small table beside his bed and at his feet, two old women appeared to be weeping.

The medicine man turned just enough letting me know he knew I was there, and then went about his business. Speaking only in their Native tongue the women began to sing a song. I was unable to understand, but somehow I knew it was words of healing. It was when I stepped closer to the bed that I realized they too were in spirit.

"My dear friend," I whispered.

Isaac smiled and gently nodded his head as he drifted off to sleep. Too many years had passed, for time had taken away his once strong shoulders, just like time had gently replaced his now greying hair.

So gentle the process that he once questioned who was staring back at him as he stoops to wash his face, a reflection in a creek expressing a time that has passed.

There was no way of knowing how long he lay there without food and water. Large green leaves (plantain) covered a large gash over his shoulder and along his arms and hands. Although they appeared to have been deep cuts, they were healing. I stayed up through the night, waking him only to offer broth made mostly of dry vegetables that I found in the cabin. The soup must have done him some good because by morning his eyes shone a little brighter.

The next few days his colour was coming back and he was sitting up. He smiled as he joked about the soup I had just made. It was what I remembered about him, his sense of humor, although you had to watch for it. It would come at the oddest time.

"You finally figured out how to catch a rabbit," Isaac said with a slight grin. He reminded me it was with the help of all the dried yellow corn he had stored. "It's what makes the rabbit stew taste so good, kanenhen:ton," he said.

A mental image came to me of Isaac drying the cooked yellow corn on the roof of his cabin, dehydrating it in the hot sun. I could still hear his voice echoing in my mind.

Shi enyókerén:onh Kanontariyo (when the snow flies it will make a good soup).

When I asked if he had seen the little girl, Isaac motioned for me to look outside. At that moment the woman in the mist appeared. She was floating inches above the ground. The woman's gentleness was shown in the child's face as she reached out taking the woman's hand.

When we first heard a little girl was lost, Sarah guided her through the beaver tunnel to keep her from harm. "Sara will take her home now," he said.

The girl had been tricked into the forest by a boy name Collin Spencer. She will not remember her ordeal.

"It was no coincidence that you entered the forest as a child. I was not sure at first, because you were at a very young age. But you are a direct bloodline and are the most pure at heart."

"How can it be when I don't have any Native blood?" I questioned.

For a long moment there was silence.

"After coming to this land," Isaac continued, "a number of my people had set out on their own, settling near small towns or villages. Some found a way to survive by offering their hunting skills to the fur traders. And others, like your great-great grandfather worked for local farmers. As years passed they were given new names, usually after their employer, and a number to work. You see no one could speak our language. Our world was changing. Only our people who remained in the forest have kept the true traditional way. You have a lot to learn and to prepare for."

My old friend then seemed a little uneasy but asked the question anyway, "When you crossed over the fence that day, tell me what happened?"

"I don't know. It just felt different," I said. "My vision became unclear like I was looking though bevelled glass. As I took another step, I felt a chill as if something or someone had brushed by me. When I turned, there was no one there."

"You were right to trust your instincts," Isaac said. "Some people say they can hear a voice in the back of their mind whenever there is danger. Most people ignore it. They're not aware they have a guide. When you were about twelve, you swam too far out into the lake. You caught a glimpse of him, your guide. Your senses were strong that day. You looked back the same instant he appeared. You quickly turned away avoiding his eyes sensing it was wrong to look at him. He warned you to go back. When you turned again, he was gone."

"Yes, I remember that day," I said.

"I never realized how far I had swum. Halfway back to shore, I didn't think I'd make it. But as quick as exhaustion took over, I felt pressure, like a hand reaching under my back keeping me afloat. It was so long ago. I never told a soul. No one would have believed it. I spent all morning looking for him, but no one came out of the water."

"How could you have known this?" I questioned Isaac.

Again there was silence! He did not answer.

"You must listen and trust only his voice because you'll have only one chance to close the gate," Isaac warned. "And know what I say is true. A Native man, not of a good mind, has removed the power from the far side of the forest selling its trees for his own greed. The forest is worth more money than he could make in a lifetime. He called himself Jim. He came to stay for a length of time when the moon was full. He showed a great interest in learning about roots and leaves for his medicine and the history of this land. His grandfather had often spoken of this forest, telling him the knowledge was here."

Jim returned again two weeks later, this time saying he yah tewakata' kari:te (wasn't well). When he left that day, lying on the ground was a pouch filled with the roots and leaves that he had collected. When I caught up to him there was something odd. There were two men stepping into the bushes, Jim and a stranger. The taller man was dressed in black, while his hat shaded his eyes.

Jim thinks this man is a friend. He has the most unsettling smile. He means him harm. I believe he is a shape shifter, but not from any clan I know. His power is like nothing I have ever seen. He can take on the form of animals or birds in an instant. I was unable to stop this man.

I had no sooner turned to go home when a huge black dog attacked me. Bleeding and exhausted from my attack I stumbled, falling down a small ravine hitting my head against a tree. When I woke, I found the bites had become infected almost immediately. But the strangest thing was my joints had stiffened so badly I could barely stand. When I arrived back at the cabin, I treated the bites as best I could and collapsed on my bed.

"You must be strong now. Remember the fear is within you, and he'll use it against you," warned Isaac.

Not of a Good Mind

Jim is a direct descendent of Smoke Watcher. His father and his father before him were taught and lived the traditional way, but not Jim. When his father found work in the city, his teaching stopped. There was so much to see and do and his teaching didn't seem interesting any more, he argued with his rohsótha' (grandfather) that day.

"To ni: yoht kiken orihwa tekarihwatenyes tsi nikarihwes konnhe?" (How are these things going to make a difference in my life?)

Jim was slowly losing respect for who he was. Slamming the back door, Jim headed to a place just outside of town, where he knew his friend Cody would be. It was no wonder they met. They shared a common feeling right from the start; they both were attracted to a small wooded lot they had seen from their apartment windows. It didn't matter how bad things got, it always felt right being close to nature. And there was one other thing they had in common. They both had families struggling to pay bills.

They talked that day of how they would like to be rich, maybe own their own company building houses. They would be able to buy anything they wanted. They walked home in silence that day, knowing in the back of their minds it was never going to happen.

"Only way to become rich is to work hard and save your money. Greed for money has caused many men and women to go to desperate measures."

Jim could still hear his rohsótha' (grandfather's) voice echoing in his mind. He knew grandfather was probably right, but that didn't stop the hunger for money, or the hope of becoming rich. As Jim lay in bed that night, months of frustration finally took its toll. Out of school over five years, how was he ever going to make something of himself? He couldn't even ask for a job. He always felt sick to his stomach becoming almost dizzy at times. He started having anxiety attacks about the same time they had moved to the city. Ro'níha (His father) would remind him from time to time that he would grow out of these attacks.

"Right!" Jim mumbled to himself.

As he reached to shut off the light next to his bed, he caught sight of the dream catcher hanging in his window. He used to like how the streetlight shone through his window, creating a silhouette. It was the last thing he saw at night, the long stream of buckskin and feathers on both sides of the circle. It used to give him a feeling of strength, a proud Nation.

Jim's mind drifted back to when he first moved to the city. He began having terrible dreams almost every night, waking up in a sweat. Always about something or someone coming to get him or trying to pull him into the darkness. It wasn't long before his mother greeted him after school with a dream catcher.

"A protection from your dreams, some even believed it could bring you good luck," his mother said. The dreams did go away and for the luck. Jim reached out pulling the dream catcher from the window and tossed into the corner of the room.

"I'll make my own ohwíhsta' (money) and it isn't going to take half a lifetime," he said.

Jim had a plan. He would remove the protection from the far side of the Sacred Forest and sell all the trees he could by entering each day behind a shield of pines and under bush, away from prying eyes. He watched his father and grandfather perform ceremonies since he was a small boy. So when Jim showed an interest, his grandfather was more than willing to tell what he knew, unaware of Jim's intentions.

"Sehyare ensatati ne ok ne'e onkwehon:we neha," (Remember you will speak only the way of the Indian) his grandfather reminded.

Jim shook his head in agreement as pride shone over his face. He knew his language. It was one thing his grandmother insisted they keep.

"The stories, the hymns, and prayers just weren't the same when spoken in any other language," she said.

Jim had released the protection from the far side of the Sacred Forest! It wasn't as if he had some kind of power. Anyone could have released the protection. Anyone with Native blood that is, but they chose not to. They all knew they would return to this land one day, if only to be laid to rest. Jim couldn't think of anything else other than how he was going to spend his money.

Jim changed that day. His anxiety was quickly replaced with self-confidence and greed. He quickly hooked up with a company that was more than willing to take him up on his offer.

But there was one other thing Jim needed to know. Once the trees and plants were gone so was the balance of what protected us. Sickness will come, in what form no one knows. As long as our people stay with traditional ways and the forest continues to be strong with growth, we are protected.

The Dark Spirit Becomes
the Stranger that Walks the Land

"Graves were now being opened and bulldozed into a heap, waking the spirits of our ancestors," Isaac said. "I first became aware that something had changed one night while I lay sleeping near the campfire. I woke with a feeling that someone was standing over me. When I turned there was no one there. I tried to go back to sleep, but the air seemed to be cooler than usual. It wasn't until I placed several logs on the fire and the flames grew higher that I saw spirits from the past coming out from the woods, e:soh nikonhti (there were many) placing themselves around the fire."

Isaac continued, "They returned each night gathering as a council. I could hear their voices without them uttering a word. Their cries were carried throughout the forest. Ne ne rotiksten'okónha' (The Old Ones) wanted to return to their resting place."

Jim had no way of knowing what took place when the gate to our land was opened. Unsure of his words, he had also opened the gate to an adjoining world. It was only for a moment before he corrected himself. But was long enough for né kanikonraksen (the Dark Spirit) to slip through creating a void for his own purpose.

Jim had released something he could never imagine, not even in his worst nightmare. It was this moment in time that the Dark Spirit had waited for. He was free to exist wherever he wanted. It was the Dark Spirit's keen sense that told him he was not alone on this land, there were others. Although, unlike his kind, these souls were similar in that they too were in spirit trapped in another existence.

Deep within the forest, far from the other burial sites laid the souls of the shape shifters. When settlers first came to our land, they greeted my people with blankets. Our people accepted them with thankful hearts not knowing a sickness came with the blankets. Some of my people had the power tsi tahatité:ni (to change), shape shift. To avoid the illness, they became birds and animals. They were different from what we knew about shape shifting. They not only became animal or bird, but they could also live within one's body.

When my ancestors found these dead animals and birds, they wrapped them inside the blankets and planted the willow trees over them. Their souls are entombed amongst the roots of the willow trees until the Creator comes for them. It was some time before they realized the blankets and bodies had to be burned to kill the disease.

But, as it happened, some of the willows were removed; né kanikonraksens (the Dark Spirit) quickly took control of them. They too want to live amongst the living. They are driven by just the power to survive, communicating with each other through their minds. They follow wherever there is a crowd pulling the warmth from the living as they brush by. Unaware of the ghostly beings, a small crowd leaving late from their festive grounds quickly complains of a cold or the flu, while they pull their sweaters and jackets tightly around them. We believe the flu symptoms, although slight, stem from the illness in the blankets that decayed beneath the willows.

Sometimes these shape shifters will find a soul who is weak or under the influence of kanekashatste (whiskey), teka'nikonhratenyes (the mind changer). Stepping into the body, they become as one, unsuspected by their families. It's the closest they're going to get to be alive again. But if they stay in the body too long, the body will become sick and death will follow.

The Shape Shifters and Strange Disappearance

"It was the Hill sisters, Valerie and Roberta that first went missing," Isaac continued.

There wasn't anything unusual about that day, maybe a little cooler than the day before. They had always enjoyed the peacefulness in the woods. The trail was wide enough for a horse and stone boat. Its path weaved in and out between the sugar maples until it made a complete circle through the woods. But once in the woods there was no way of turning back with the large spread of young maples so close together. The only other option was to walk in. They both agreed to walk to the halfway mark where the sap was boiled down. That way they would be home before dark. They quickly followed the trail already marked out for them.

Although it had been some time since the trees were tapped, they still enjoyed the fond memories of emptying the buckets of sap into a barrel with their grandfather. It was Valerie who became concerned when they didn't find the fire pit.

"Just keep walking the trail. It won't take us anywhere but out," Roberta reminded.

When the trail ended abruptly and the only path in front of them was created by nature's runoff, Roberta took it all in stride. "Where is all your adventure?" she said laughingly.

Reluctantly, Valerie followed her sister down a ravine where they could see a small shack. The greying timbers looked to be a hundred years old.

"I don't remember grandfather ever saying that anyone even lived way out here," Valerie said as she grabbed her sister's arm.

"We'll be fine. We'll just take a quick look," Roberta said.

The missing pane and dirty glass only reassured Roberta that no one lived there. A snake slithered between the tall weeds as they released the door latch. Dust was everywhere and it was clear to see why some of the floorboards had buckled. Just overhead was a large hole in the roof. Seeing that no one lived there any more Roberta's excitement to explore heightened. The chair with no back gave Roberta an extra step up to see what was in the attic.

"Just some old buckets," she said as she stepped down.

"There's another room here," Valerie said as she made a gesture for Roberta to follow. Valerie quickly stepped back. "I just saw a man, a tall man, she stutters. He's sitting there on that old bed frame. We got to get out of here," Valerie whispered anxiously.

"But there's no one here," Roberta said.

Valerie knew what she saw. It was at this moment that Valerie noticed shadows were appearing in the room, the sun was setting.

"We've stayed too long," Valerie said while she hurried to open the outside door in hopes her sister would quickly follow.

But just as the door flung open, about fifty feet from the cabin stood three huge black dogs. Their odd movements suggested they were waiting.

"We have no choice but to wait it out here," Roberta said. "Don't worry, we're safe here," she assures.

At the same time, she was searching the cabinet for any kind of protection. Suddenly their skin began to crawl as chills ran up their backs.

It was Roberta who screamed, "Don't turn around. Don't look at him. He's not real. He can't harm us."

She was half right. Roberta watched in horror as the dogs pushed their way through the open door. It was here they witnessed the dogs stand upright on their hind legs. A dark mist pulled itself from their bodies while the dogs crumpled against the floor. Valerie stood limp, her arms hung loose at her side. Her eyes stared blankly.

"They can't harm us," Roberta shouted as she tried to keep control. But she was defenseless as fear took command.

"When they woke, two days had passed. They were found stumbling down a long road covered in dirt as if they had burrowed themselves out of the ground with no memory of how they got there. We believe it was Roberta's strong will and perseverance that saved her and her sister," Isaac said.

It was only after weeks had passed; slowly the trauma of that night began to waken. Lost in this unknown darkness, their minds struggled to shake their confusion. Tangled roots seemed to be everywhere. It was that caged in feeling where terror began to fill their souls. Their arms immediately thrashed out at anything in their way.

It was when Roberta heard her sister's cries the confusion was lifted. And it was the sandy soil that began to trickle down just above them that pulled at every substance of Roberta's soul, setting off the reaction to survive. Their only hope was to follow the faint smell of cedar, that and the fresh soil that seemed to be filling in around then.

In a loud whisper Roberta urges Valerie to push away any loose soil that she could. The smell of cedar was right above them. They desperately fought to escape as fresh air filled their lungs.

It was also the two Hill sisters that had seen Jacoby Woods along a path in the same forest that fateful night, while they scrambled to find their way out of this unknown forest. Jacoby's steps were unsteady, his arms hung awkwardly at his side while he seemed to be following close behind two large dogs.

Roberta and Valerie didn't know why they were in this part of the wood or how they got there. The only thing they did know, they both felt a great urgency to leave this forest as quickly as possible.

Jacoby also caught a glimpse of the two sisters as they hid behind some bushes along the path, but couldn't grasp what was wrong. He tried to shake the fuzzy feeling in his head. Why were these women in the woods in the middle of the night? At that moment, his mind shut down, the shape shifter now had complete control.

Jacoby had traveled Old Highway 24 many times on his way back home. He was an entrepreneur of sorts, selling kitchen gadgets from town to town out of the trunk of his car. It was about three in the morning, hardly any vehicles on the road, and he was looking forward to a week of rest.

Maybe it was the long road he had just travelled that made him take the next side road home, cutting the remaining travel time in half. He hadn't driven very far when he saw something moving in the ditch straight ahead of him. Some kind of animal he thought. He quickly wiped the front window with his sleeve to get a better look. Kicking himself at that moment, as he recalls his wife scolding him to clean the brownish film that had gummed up on his window from years of smoking in his car. It was here that a dog sprang up out of the ditch and leaped in front of his headlights, a hairless dog. Its torso and legs were not of a dog, but of a man. Swerving to miss this animal, he lands the back end of his car in the opposite ditch.

Uninjured, he quickly grabbed his flashlight as he scouted around the area, but there was nothing there. Jacoby had no choice but to walk for help. He hadn't walked very far when he heard something coming behind him.

A faint voice called out, "Wait up."

Jacoby quickly turns, but again there was no one there. And for a moment he could feel his heart racing at the suddenness of hearing a voice in the darkness. Shining the light along the ditch, he called out.

"Who's there?"

A voice replied, "May I walk with you for a while? And can you turn off the light. It hurts my eyes."

When Jacoby turned the light off, a tall figure of a man appeared from the ditch. As they walked on, the man began to tell Jacoby of a card game that was going on just ahead of them.

"It's just around the next bend about half mile away, there I will find a ride for you." the stranger coaxed.

Jacoby felt certain, and appreciated the help the tall man was offering, he would be home before daylight. Suddenly, Jacoby could hear a rush of footsteps along the ditch. He quickly fumbled to turn on his flashlight, but again there was no one there. It was only when he checked closer that he saw the dogs crawling on their bellies in the lowest part of the ditch. Dark shadows began to leap back and forth across the road as if they were playing a game with him.

When they found Jacoby's body two weeks later, the coroner asked the next of kin if he suffered from arthritis. His joints had swollen so badly his bones began to separate.

Isaac Heeds a Great Warning

Every nine days the kanikonraksen (Dark Spirit) (the Stranger) must return to regenerate. And with every nine days the shape shifters will enter into the Stranger's world releasing captive souls, atónnhets í:ken atónnhets (a soul for a soul). With this process, the shape shifters must then return to the depth of the willows each day, always before the sun rises. When the time is right, the Stranger will release his kind upon the earth.

You must seal their tomb and close the void before it's too late. The more he controls, the more powerful he will become. They travel along the back roads at night and they fear no one.

A Calculated Meeting

It was on this long stretch of road Jim first met the Stranger. Staying late after a party, Jim and Cody stood speechless as they looked out the back door, somehow missing the only ride they had back to town. It seemed Jim and his friend Cody were always the last to leave. Jim did admit that night to having too much to drink and he laughed when his friend Cody warned him not to walk on the road at night, especially in the fog.

"There is always the couch or the floor, Jim," Cody shouted from the doorway.

Jim gave a slight grin as he wearily took a seat on an oversized log just in front of the house. He smiled to himself as he remembered it had stopped many of his friends from driving through the front window as their cars failed to come to a complete stop. Jim didn't know if it was lack of money to fix the brakes or the lack of know-how. He smiled again at their recklessness and teetered just a little as he bent down to tie his shoelace.

Jim never thought much about the old stories Cody's grandfather had told them about hearing bones rattling

along the path to the river. And at that same time he remembered his own grandfather telling him how his father
had rushed the family indoors one foggy night. An unusual
spring thaw had come early that late February, making it
almost impossible to see what was walking near them. Unbelievable story, as great grandfather raced his family inside to put out any flame in fear the bone rattlers would see
a light and come and take a family member.

"That story about the fog. It was probably passed
down for hundreds of years," Jim said as a smirk fell across
his face.

"But they might be back," Cody warned. "The Elders
are saying something's not right. Our people are gathering
from all over, returning to their home communities. They feel
a great urgency to go back to the Sacred Forest, their homes.
And there's one more thing Jim, the spirits of our ancestors
are being sighted. They're coming in this direction."

"No more stories! I've got to get home," Jim said.

And he let out several high pitched wailing cries! An
old Indian war cry and threw his fist in to the air.

Cody quickly followed his lead. It was their way of
reminding themselves of who they were - a bloodline of
great warriors.

Jim's arms quickly fell to his sides while his legs
wobbled beneath him. Jim didn't have a care in the world.
He had walked this length of road many times. And besides
the moon was full, and if he had any problems he would
knock at one of the old farmhouses along the way. But just
as he left the warm comforting light and stepped into the
darkness, a sudden loud screech of an owl startled him as
it swooped down barely missing his right ear. And for just
a moment he could have sworn he heard né tsihstékerih'
wa'tkatsyáhon (the owl whisper). Jim laughed dismissively
as he tried to walk a steady pace. But the further he walked,
the more he thought about another story his grandfather
had told him.

One night his grandfather had taken a walk, and on his return an owl also flew so close he could have sworn he too had heard a faint whisper. His grandfather warned someone close had died. The next day his grandfather had spoken of the death of a good friend.

Jim suddenly felt a cold chill run up his back. Maybe he should get off the road. In the distance, he could see a small light glowing from a farmhouse window, although it seemed odd there would be anyone up at that hour. He had understood a farmer went to bed early and rose at the break of day. He quickly climbed over the fence that now stood in front of him. His steps were uneven as he rushed to make it before the light when out. He hadn't gone very far when he stumbled. It was here that he felt a hand reach out of the darkness pulling him to his feet. A tall man stepped forward.

His voice echoed in the stillness, "Looks like you need a little help my friend."

Jim thought it was odd that this man was in the field at that late hour. He strained to see what this tall man looked like. The man's oddness quickly disappeared when the Stranger coaxed Jim to come along and join his friends in the nearby house for one last drink. The closer Jim got to the old house the slower his steps became.

"Onkwathón:te'ne' tsyok nahò:ten wa:waks," (I just heard something rattle) Jim said. In that same instant Jim already knew what he just heard, it was the sound of bones.

"I heard you say you wanted to be rich," the Stranger said, as they stepped into the darkened house.

A spine-chilling presence confirmed what Jim was already thinking. "Sometimes evil is standing right beside him!"

When Jim woke the next day, he was lying in his own bed.

As the days followed, his mother began to see a change in Jim, but had convinced herself it was just the flu.

It was Cody who had a bad feeling. There was something about that night. After the party, he had stood outside the house waiting for Jim to return. He was almost certain he would come running up the road, especially after he heard that blood-curdling scream in the distance. It was the most piercing cry he had ever heard, almost like the sound of a lynx. It couldn't have been anything other, he told himself. He heard they made a sound almost like a human screaming, like someone trapped in some kind of vice.

The dense fog also played a part in searching for Jim. The fog came up almost immediately after Jim left, circling the house. All Cody could do was hope he made it home.

After about a week or so of not getting any return calls from Jim, and hearing Jim's mother's concern about his odd behavior, working late into the night and having these flu symptoms during the day and that awful scream still fresh in Cody's mind, Cody had to see for himself. When he opened the bedroom door, he couldn't believe what he saw. Jim looked to be in shock. Whatever happened that night, Jim was a part of it. His arms and stomach seemed to be bruised from the inside, his eyes unclear. When Jim tried to stand, it was noticeably awkward. His hands fumbled about as he tried to push himself upward from the bed. His body resembled an old man's. When Cody asked if he was all right, he made a complete turn while his eyes strained to find Cody in the room.

"He was shaking all over, the morning he came home and making no sense," Jim's mother said as she entered the room.

She even went so far as to say it was the stress of his business. Jim was buying up all the land he could, of course under false pretenses, and selling its trees sometimes even before he signed the deed, with no thought for the future.

"Some business," Isaac said as he hung his head in shame.

One Chance to Complete the Task

Too much time has passed. You must reach the willows in one given day at the precise time when the willows are still. There is a great connection between these souls and the willows. As far back as I can remember, yah nonwenton yah teyaonnhe:yonh kiken kerhiton ton (these trees have never died). Rake'níha (My father) often spoke of the willows, as his father did. Tsi nikariwehs ne yowerathsaste sewatye:ren ensathontene tehonhshenthos. (Sometimes you can hear their cries when the wind is strong). The wind has a natural way to remind us that shape shifters are still there.

My ancestors tried to undo what had happened. They unearthed the bones of the animals and birds the shape shifters had become. My ancestors then tried to burn their bones into ashes to release their souls. But with the heavy rain that followed that day, their ashes seeped into the young willows. The willows are just as much a part of them. You must seal their resting place and close the void before the next transition. Follow the creek till you come to a grove of willows. It is here that the shape shifters will return each day, just before dawn.

The ceremony must be completed without delay. There will be no second chance. When you have sealed the tomb, you must return to the path and continue to the boulders. Remember to always stay within the sound of the creek.

The passage between the two worlds will be visible only when the morning sun casts its first light. Look for the eye of the boulder. It will guide you to the gate. The Stranger will return at exactly the same time every nine days. Once he steps into its depth, you must complete the words that were given to you with no hesitation.

"Remember," Isaac continued. "Keep an eye on any high branches. Look for any unusual behavior from the birds and animals. Be especially careful of any dogs. Watch your back. They crawl on their bellies, waiting for their chance."

The Old Woman Along the Creek

I left early the next morning still rehearsing my lines as if going off to a play, a play from which I might never return. As I made my way down a small ravine, I could see the path that fell along the creek while it twisted and turned through the woods. It was different in this part of the forest. Huge trees were everywhere. This was the oldest part of the forest. Vines were strewn about from one tree to the next entwining the branches like a web. The thick thorn bushes were making it almost impossible to stay on the path. I would crawl under where I could. It was only when I spotted droppings that I realized the path was an old animal trail that lay directly along the creek. I would not sleep through the night and would arrive just before dawn.

The full moon lit up the night as it hung directly above my right shoulder. Long thin branches draping over the path resembled the shape of fingers, making the stillness of the night seem even more eerie. It wasn't anything other than branches, but still the sight made me think the worst. Staying on the path, I came to a large tree. It must have recently rained for the weight of the tree had given way to the marsh. Its leaves still soft to the touch. It was here that I crossed the creek. This trail here seemed to be worn down by more than just animals.

Cautiously I continued along the way until the trail forked in two directions. I would stay on course. But it was when I took another step that I noticed a small flickering light in the opposite direction. The glowing light was captivating while it lured me through the darkness. I hungered to see anyone. Every sound was becoming a warning. Just a glimpse I told myself.

Cautiously, I made my way through the bushes, crouching down I watched as a Native woman stood alone tending to her fire. Her movement became unsteady as she seated herself on a log a few feet from the fire, her hands immediately reached out catching its warmth. But it was the smell of food cooking that drew my curiosity even closer.

When I called out to her, she quickly covered her face but did not answer. I stood alongside her trying to persuade her not to be afraid of me. When she turned, I gasped at the sight in front of me. The whites of her eyes seemed to be illuminated against the brightness of the fire. She was blind. I would not learn her name for some time or how she came to be there. She kept her distance, while I tried to convince her to come along.

Emily

Emily was a superstitious woman, and I guess you would be too if you had heard and seen the things she had seen in her lifetime. She came from a culture of storytellers, stories passed down from one generation to the next. But some stories were not often spoken of. Witchcraft, some believed these witches still lived among the different clans. And if she knew anything about her customs, she knew there was one thing you did not do. And that was to tell anyone, when you suspected someone was practicing witchcraft. What had happened to her couldn't be anything else. She would stay silent.

Emily had first met the Stranger on her way home, after staying late to clean up after a gathering with her friends. Still enough hours in the day and it wasn't uncommon to see Emily walking alone on the road. Twice a month, she would hitchhike into the neighbouring town. She didn't know what the whispering was all about or why they pulled their children away as she walked by. She'd pick up her bag of flour, point her finger at them and in her Native tongue she would scold.

"Tokat tsi nahò:ten' sherihenyen:nis nene eksa'okónha, oh ne nahòten ronennonhtonnyons nene rati-kónhsa'seh-
son?" (If this is what you are teaching your children, what
will the new generation be like?)

But on this particular day, she felt good about the
world. Her energy was high after spending the afternoon
with her friends, and maybe this was why her guard was
down. She hadn't walked very far when a truck pulled up
alongside her. With the Stranger's good looks and charm,
Emily felt at ease as she climbed into the front seat, and
agreed to come along while he made another stop about
half a mile down the road.

"He's just a young man, having some trouble along
the way. It won't take too long," the Stranger said.

Emily felt a little uneasy when the Stranger pulled
into a dirt road leading into the woods, fearful when the
road in front of them suddenly took a sharp turn behind
some heavy bushes and pine trees making the view impossible to see from the main road. Her fears quickly turned to
anger, when he refused to stop the truck to let her out. A
feisty woman when she was mad, no one was going to tell
her what to do.

"Wakatitahkwenh eh ki' nón:weh (I'll get out right
here)! Just pull over," she demanded. "Enkathahine eh
tkiteren." (I'll walk to my home.)

But it was too late. She was here for the ride through
miles of bush. At times the trail was barely wide enough to
pass through. Then suddenly the truck swerved as the back
tires hit the freshly turned soil. When the dust cleared, all
she could see were mounds of roots heaved up in a pile drying against the sun, acre upon acre, clear cutting.

Angry, the Stranger slowly released his grip on the
steering wheel. His nostrils flared as he roughly pulled
Emily from the truck.

"I guess you got your wish," he said as he leans forward his unearthly dark eyes now inches from hers. And

for an instant she questioned who she had been riding with. "Weren't his eyes green as she climbed up into his truck."

At that moment she could feel his grip tighten as he began to pull her through the thick undergrowth, where they continued on through the thickest part of the forest. He knew just where he was going, stopping just in front of a grove of weeping willows. She also knew this place or the story behind it. When she was just a young girl, she and her friends would often sneak outside and huddle together in an old abandoned building, telling stories of the willows.

"Ohniyotyé:renh senòn:wes kiken kerhi'ton:ton?" (Why do you like these trees?) Emily said to the Stranger, as she tried to stop her voice from shaking. "No one ever comes here."

"It's what's beneath the trees," he said, and quickly grabbed Emily's arm securing her next to him.

"The ceremony can only be spoken in the onkwehón:weh tsi nikawenno:ton (Native language) and I don't believe you know the language," she said, as she stared up at him in her smug little way.

She was fluent in her Mohawk language!

It was here Emily saw something she had only seen once before, his appearance was changing. Dark shadows now traced his once pleasant features, and his black eyes seem to look right through her. It was with his strange appearance she knew her very existence was in danger.

What happened after that seemed to be a little unclear, but one thing she did remember, she fought with all her strength to no avail. The tall Stranger had taken her sight, for what she had seen. When she woke, the warmth of the sun was high. Afraid to shout for help in fear they would return, she stumbled along trying to find her way back to the main road. It was when she found an old fire pit in a small clearing that she stopped in hopes a hiker might return.

Surviving with her hunting skills, it was nothing for Emily to fasten a snare together with what she could find, catching a rabbit every time. It was part of her family tradition. It had been as far back as she could remember to spend a week or two in the woods with just a knife and the clothes on her back.

The Willows

There's a reason why I met this sightless woman, although I couldn't think how she could help me. It wasn't part of the plan. She would probably slow me down, but I knew I couldn't just leave her here.

"You must trust your instinct," Isaac had said.

These words were still going through my mind as I started to guide Emily along the path. She seemed to know there was urgency as her pace quickened. We walked in silence while our ears pulled at the slightest sound. They would be returning to their resting place. It was inevitable. Just like the hours would turn to minutes before we knew it, and the sun would rise as usual.

"Try to stay on the path," I whispered. "Something just brushed by my leg."

I had no sooner said these words than two dark shadows stepped out onto the path, huge black dogs. These once feared dogs now looked as if they had fought the battle of all battles, too weak to even care we were there. They had come back to rest.

We kept our distance while others stepped onto the path, some in human form, while another had not quite changed. Its pale skin stood out against the moonlight – the head of a dog while his back a torso of a man. Their steps were in a slow and uneven pace. I watched as the arms of the willows parted and they, one by one, vanished into the depth of the darkness.

As soon as I felt it was safe, we hurried to the opening. Emily instinctively scurried around in her blindness finding sticks and dead branches for a fire. Taking the pouch from my belt, I watched the smoke rise as a sudden wind carried the scent of their oyen'kwa'ón:weh (traditional tobacco) through the air as it circled the willows. It was now time, but something was wrong.

I began to fumble over my words and yet I knew them. Strangely I began to feel their presence as if they were right beside me, and in the next instant, I felt my spirit being pulled from me, down into its depth. If I didn't act now, we would be a part of them.

"Kahkwíhsrons (Try harder), just try to remember," Emily was shouting.

I didn't have time to even wonder why she could now speak. I drew in a deep breath while a sudden stillness ran through me. When I turned, a man stood just behind me. His hair was a brilliant yellow. A familiar voice echoed in my mind as I found myself for an instant swimming back in the lake. My words now flowed with confidence, as I could hear his every word. Suddenly, a scream pierced my ears.

"My name is Emily. I know who he is. I've seen the Stranger."

Emily fell to her knees, as she fought once more to erase the painful memory of that night, but her mind wouldn't let her. Her healing had begun. Her mind's eye quickly took her back seizing that day. The air was stagnating as she and the Stranger arrived at the willows. Emily watched as the sun slowly dimmed its light casting a bluish grey haze as far as she could see. A presence of despair seemed to be in this place as the willows hung lifeless, worn down from time that had past. But when a sudden cold wind blew in waking the willows, their long thin branches seemed to rejoice as they danced along the ground in celebration of the Stranger's arrival.

Overwhelmed with what was taking place, Emily watched in horror while a number of trees fell leaving a large crater in the ground. It was here that the tall Stranger dragged Emily screaming and kicking, threatening to drop her just over the edge, entombing her soul forever if she didn't do his bidding. Without her knowledge of her language, these souls were useless to him. She complied, unaware what her freedom would cost.

She was helpless against his strength. In her torment, she reached out at the last moment seizing a branch with all her might. Tossed from his sight she lay motionless, her fist still clinging onto some leaves. Finding something so small, so familiar, she needed to feel its existence, something that could be explained, for what had happened to her couldn't have been real. She was blind.

It wasn't till now that Emily remembered finding seeds in her pocket and the verse did say the seeds of the willow. Emily quickly reached into her pocket and tossed the seeds down into the darkness. Within moments the earth heaved up. Large trees sprouted up everywhere sealing the tomb.

Emily stood in silence and for a long moment while she gazed up into the sky. She seemed to gain strength as I watched her shoulders broaden against the light of the fire. Slowly, she turned and smiled. "Í:kens ne Kerhi'tó:tonh (I see the standing trees) I'm ok now," she said in a loud whisper.

The Faceless Rock

Time was critical as we didn't know the distance we still had to travel. It was Emily's keen sense of hearing that alerted us in the direction of a crow perched high in a distant tree. We were closer than we thought. My heart quickened as we raced in its direction, but all that stood in front of us was a large ravine. Hundreds of trees littered the banks of the once active gorge etched some thousands of years ago. Only a small creek remained. Its source forever changed for the sake of development.

A measurement of time, I had no way of knowing the minutes we had left. But just when we had lost all hope, we sighted three large stones at the edge of the bank all similar in size. With its odd location, we quickly climbed down to see if it was what we thought it was. Nestled in its bank stood two gigantic boulders while the three rounded stones seem to grace its top. I stood looking up at these faceless rocks. There was no eye anywhere. But just as the sun had shed its first light and the forest had cast its first shadow, I caught a glimpse of the sun's rays as they pierced between the boulders. And for a second I could see what my old friend was talking about. It did resemble an eye!

As the sun rose so did its strength. The eye sent out a light so brilliant the boulders seemed to part. And I watched as a sliver of light emerged from beneath the ground. Its brightness was fused by thousands of lost souls. When the light faded, I looked into its depth. I stood in awe as I watched the torment in their hollow faces. Their screams forever unheard, soul after soul passed in front of me like leaves being pulled along on a brisk autumn day only to be gathered up yet again in its distance. Lost for eternity without a reason why!

The Old Ones

It was Emily who pulled me from this hypnotic world as she shouted just behind me. "ronónha' kèn:thoh" (They're here)! "Rotihskenhrakéhteh" (the warriors). "The Old Ones," Emily shouted again, "they're all around us!"

When I turned, I saw with great amazement the spirits of our ancestors.

"I had heard in certain times," Emily continued, her voice had now lowered, "my people would see né rotiksten'okónha' (The Old Ones), sometimes guiding them to safety or forewarning them of danger, but nothing like this. They're saying they won't leave us."

Emily's voice was now trembling, and in the same instant I too wondered what was in store for us. Hearing branches snapping just behind us, we quickly turned to see a large buck stepping down onto this small clearing where we now stood. His nostrils were flaring while his chest heaved in an uneven rhythm. Our steps immediately coincided as we stepped back heeding the danger in front of us. Our eyes quickly caught the distance below securing our safety if we had to jump. Emily quickly grabbed my arm.

"It's a shape shifter," she whispered.

"This animal was not new to this part of the forest. I've seen him before. He must have followed me right from the start," I said.

"This ceremony can't be done on animals. We'll have to wait till he's in human form," Emily whispered.

"We might not have time," I said and pointed in the direction of the boulder. "Snakes!" I whispered. "They are everywhere."

I watched in horror, as they pushed up through the ground all around me. Dozens more slithered down from the edge of the bank until they resembled a huge ball at the foot of the boulder. My knees buckled as I tried desperately to keep my sense about me.

"I'm deathly afraid of snakes," I whispered.

"Ónyarehsoń'a" (snakes), Emily repeated.

It was at that moment Jim staggered into our midst. His eyes were clear now, free from the soul that lived within him, but it was too late. He would be dead before the day was over. He could feel his flesh literally tearing from his bones with each step he took. He fought with every ounce of life he had left, just to be here.

Jim knew he was in trouble the morning he woke from the party. He couldn't remember anything after he stepped into that old farmhouse. As the days passed, he could feel his body crippling. His head at times would wobble uncontrollably, like the old man ro'níha (his Dad) had visited in the nursing home in town. He was burning up with a fever all day. At night, he was freezing almost to a point where he thought he would die, but the strangest part was waking up in the forest beneath the willows.

Jim fought every day to keep his strength and his sanity. He had no control over what was happening to him. He tried desperately to tell his mother and his friend Cody, but his words weren't making sense. This was Jim's last chance to redeem himself for what he so carelessly took from our territory.

Jim stepped up to the boulders and proceeded to pick up the snakes like you would pick up a pile of laundry and tossed them down the remaining bank.

Visibly weakened, the tall Stranger lunged forward ridding himself from the large buck. The buck instinctively pulled back, away from his intruder, his strong legs quickly carried him up and away from the bank with ease.

But it was with each transition, the Stranger would become physically ill. Even though he needed the birds and animals for his sight and their ability to travel, their flesh sickened him. He was powerless now.

It was only by chance the Dark Spirit had seen this opening to this world. Hidden in the darkness, he had watched as a man had entered his world, his soul untouched by death. His long black hair reached the end of his back, a strong physical man carrying only his bow and knife. Fueled by his anger, his strength became even stronger as he fought the deep cold of this underworld. He vows to retrieve his brother's soul. This man hastily vanished into the darkness.

It would be two hundred years before the Dark Spirit would have that chance again.

When Jim opened the gate to the Sacred Forest that day, the Dark Spirit quickly slipped through. Stepping out onto the unfamiliar land, he found himself among a race of people he knew nothing about. The unseen spirit would walk among these people and learn their ways. They seemed unchanged by the ever-growing world that stood all round them, depicting a better life. A Nation of people living on just a fragment of what land they once had, driven from their homeland, surviving through hunger and sickness, a proud Nation. They believed they were placed on earth to protect the forest and the precious plants that lived within, a belief that hadn't changed for thousands of years.

The Dark Spirit seemed satisfied with himself knowing what he knew. Keep this race of people down long enough, the greed for money will outweigh their importance.

In the not so distant future, this land and their race would be gone. Large towering buildings would take their place.

These people were of no interest to him, but what did intrigue the Dark Spirit was learning about the souls that could live in one's body, controlling their every thought. With this knowledge, he headed in the direction of the willows. His only intention was to control these souls to do his bidding so others like himself could pass through from his world - a soul for a soul.

It was the Dark Spirit's good fortune when he spotted a young man on a back road changing a flat tire. A rather tall man lifted the worn out tire with ease and tossed it in the back of his truck. His shoulder broadened just a little as he boasted to himself on a job well done. It would be the last sane thought the young man would have. The Dark Spirit needed his existence, but something was different. He found he could keep this human body alive, regenerating it every nine days unlike the souls of the shape shifters. Once they possess one's body, the human ceases to regenerate. Within days the body will cripple up and death would slowly follow!

With the Stranger's (the Dark Spirit) plan, he knew in just a short time the shape shifter would have enough souls to complete his plan. These ghostly beings would rise to walk upon the earth, and cities would fall because of them.

An old man now stood near the boulders. I looked in disbelief as the Stranger's back had suddenly curved and his skin had weathered some fifty years. The Stranger knew in his weakened condition, this body and his soul couldn't exist in this world. In his last attempt to save himself, he leaped into Jim's sickened body. Within seconds Jim's body collapsed to the ground as the dark mass wrenched Jim's soul into its hellish depth.

Our ears were filled with Jim's torment. Our minds fought desperately to block out the mental image of Jim's suffering.

With no time to waste, we quickly lit the ceremonial fire, and we watched as the smoke carried the scent of oyen'kwa'hón:weh (traditional tobacco) into the air. For the final prayer would be given. But it was the rotiksten'okónha (Old Ones) who perceived the Stranger was not quite gone. Emily and Beth watched as the Old Ones take to the sky circling the unearthly demons, as they heaved up from the gate of the underworld. Hundreds more ghostlike warriors fill the gorge beneath them with their war clubs raised high. Emily and I watched in horror as the warriors fought in triumph driving the demons down into their hellish depth.

And when the final words were spoken, I felt the earth tremble. I watched the boulders shake with a force so strong they toppled onto the ground sealing the passage. And one by one the Old Ones vanished, their shoulders stooped from the weight of exhaustion.

Physically and mentally drained, I fell to my knees. Emily stood in silence while tears welled up in her eyes. She just had the fright of her life and at the same instant she was bursting with pride, proud that the Old Ones were still watching over her people. And for an unknown time, we sat looking out over the ravine lost in an understood silence. In the next instant, I watched as Emily fell back against the ground, her arm immediately shields the sun while her mind finds sleep as exhaustion take its toll and for a long moment I too let my eyes close. We felt the warmth of the sun as it fell against our skin, for our healing had begun.

It was the cry of a distant crow that broke the stillness that lay over the land reminding me we still had a long walk home. We both agreed it would be best to stay the night at the old campsite where we first met.

Part Two

When Beth returned to the forest, she found her friend Isaac gravely ill. He believed the dog that had attacked him that day wasn't all what it seemed to be, but a man, a stranger to this land. Isaac had seen this tall dark figure step from behind some heavy bushes; in seconds a dog had attacked him.

In the darkness, along a well-travelled path Beth befriends a blind woman named Emily. Fearing for Emily's safety, Beth takes her along as she undertakes what had to be done - to seal the shape shifters back into their tomb beneath the willows. All the while keeping in mind she must arrive at first light to seal the gate to the underworld before it's too late. A simple task, she thought. But something was at hand here. After several attempts to re-member the verse given to her by Isaac, Beth could feel her very soul being pulled from her, as she fought to remember the verse.

It was in this same moment, a golden haired man appeared, a memory from her childhood of a long forgotten messenger who warned her of the deep water over half a lifetime ago. Knowing the unseen hand had kept her afloat long ago as she fought against the water. A trust she knew. The Mohawk language now flowed as gentle as a whisper just behind Beth's ear as she recited the verse.

Shakwarihwanonton:nihs shonkwayatihson (We ask you Creator) i:ken nisóshatstenhsero:ten (for it is indeed your strength you have), askerhitahara:tate (to uplift the trees) in their natural order. Satennyehthha ne yóaweyen tsi ashehnekanónten (send the morning dew for watering) ase sanenhon tyon (the new seeds I have planted). Sha kwarihwanonton:nihs yohterahwatase (We ask you to bind the roots with a strong hold) tsi niyore tentahsewe (until you come again).

In the next instant, they watched the trees stand upright as if by unseen hands. The ground trembled as the earth fell back into place, sealing the shape shifters beneath the willows. Again fate would intervene as they struggled to seal the opening to the underworld, so loud were the mournful cries as the ghostly demons pulled themself free. It was here that the Old Ones take to the sky forcing the ghostly demons back down into their hellish depth.

Exhausted from their ordeal Beth and Emily agree to make camp where they first met.

Beth and Emily Return
to the Campsite

While following the trail back to the campsite where Emily and I first met, the air felt as if it had renewed itself, like it had rained the night before. Still my thoughts were heavy as I tried to make light of what happened only hours ago. It seemed unbelievable, as my mind continued to relive what I had seen. The boulder not only toppled onto the gate of the underworld, the boulder was concealed when a large section of the cliff mysteriously broke away. Spirits, how was it even possible that hundreds of spirits could materialize right in front us. When I turned to Emily, she was staring up at me as if she knew what I was about to ask.

"No one can explain why some of our people are able to see these ghostlike spirits. We believe they are always there, coexisting, parallel with our world. It is only in troubled times or times of danger that they become visible. Some forms are so vivid, we could swear they are real. The only difference is they don't speak. Their voices are heard in our thoughts, as if we are hearing their words coming to us from a distance."

Time seemed to pass by quickly as Emily spoke of her beliefs. When we arrived, the fire pit was covered over with dirt that I had kicked onto the remaining embers the night before. Our tracks leading to the campsite suggested no one had been here.

Pulling the strap from my shoulder, I mentally thanked Isaac for the dried venison he had insisted I take along. I smiled to myself as I recalled seeing Isaac taking one of the several leather pouches that were strewed along the wall in his cabin and began slapping the pouches against his pant leg as dust flew into the air. At that moment I reached into the pouch and took two larger pieces to share with Emily. The site was different from what I remembered with the low fire burning the night before. But the flames were high enough to cast strange shadows that seemed to be forming behind the surrounding trees. For a moment, I found myself looking for familiar objects matching things I had only seen in the darkness.

Uncomfortable feelings crept over me as I recalled finding Emily here alone and the shock of learning that she was blind through some kind of curse or magic. And for the life of me, I couldn't ask her about the torment she must have gone through at the hands of the Stranger, the Dark Spirit from the underworld.

For a moment a slight smile fell across my face knowing I had played a small part in restoring her eyesight. It happened when I recited a verse given to me by Isaac, while he was recovering at his home. It was a verse that could only be spoken in the Mohawk language. I had disagreed with Isaac that day. There was no way I could learn his language in so little time. Although the verse was not that long, I couldn't believe how easily I picked up his dialect, and I couldn't have imagined what power these words would have.

I shudder to think what would have happened if it wasn't for the help of a golden haired man that stood behind me guiding me through the ceremony, when I mysteriously forgot the verse given to me. Something was at hand here.

With the memories still fresh in my head, I let my mind pull me along as I recalled the willows mysteriously standing back up, as if by large ghostlike hands. These unseen hands continued in my mind filling the reason why the ground around them continued to shake as the earth fell into place, sealing the shape shifters back in their tomb.

A story, I wouldn't have even thought possible, but something had changed in this forest since that first day I had entered as a child, as well as inside myself. I never believed I was superstitious, but the things I had just witnessed in the last twenty-four hours continued to eat at my mind.

The self-confidence I felt about myself the day I stepped back into this forest was now troubled. I was shaken. This world wasn't all that I believed it was. Knowing what I know now, I would not have stepped into this forest. Something inside me told me to stay silent.

"What I don't know can't hurt me."

Emily Gives Warning
of this Strange World

Emily began stomping her feet as if she was knocking the snow from her boots. I turned to see her remove the last piece of coal from the fire pit as she tossed it to the side with the toe of her boot. Emily made a crooked smile when I saw her pick up a handful of dirt from the ground. She continued rubbing the sandy soil till most of the soot was gone from her boots and hands.

Emily then seemed lost in her thoughts while staring down at the twigs and small branches she had been arranging.

"We must always remember they are not all kanikon:rihyo (good spirits)," Emily said as she spoke again of her beliefs. "My father, as well as my grandparents had often warned my brothers and sister as well as myself not to walk alone at night. Some people say they can hear footsteps along the road following them at night, but when they turn there is no one there. Many believe the bad medicine that was practiced hundreds of years ago had drawn kanikon raksens (bad spirits) into our world.

Ceremonies may have been left open or they were unsure of their words. It was known by our people not to practice bad medicine. It was only to be used if all else failed and only a handful would know this knowledge. Most of our people won't have anything to do with these things. We can never trust what will come through once the passage is open. Some of these spirits can influence our way of thinking. Occasionally, our people are able to send them back to their world, but the ceremonies are hard to do and it can be very risky. Sometimes the spirits follow you home. The dark shadows, or kahòn:tish (black) tyaonhawi:non (mist) as some describe it, are the most feared."

Emily's head pulled slightly back as she studied Beth's face for the common expression that she had seen before.

"In my culture it isn't unusual to see and hear these things," Emily reminded Beth.

Emily again hesitated, as she seemed to be pre-occupied with her thoughts. She immediately scanned the brushes and high branches and began to laugh jokingly.

"I guess I'm feeling a little spooked talking about these things. Maybe that's a good thing. It will give me an edge," she laughs.

Emily was a person that I wouldn't soon forget. She seemed to have toughness about her, a resilience to bounce back. She found humour in the obstacles in front of her and in a person's reason. She did remind me a lot of Isaac in that he studied what I was saying, finding my meaning before he answered. At first, I thought he was cross. His stern face and dark eyes prevented me from seeing the gentleness in him, as well as in Emily.

Emily is a petite woman. Her leathery brown skin told me she spends a lot of time outdoors. Maybe she's a vegetable farmer, I thought. Years of working the land in the hot sun was visibly etched in her face, showing the hard labour she had endured in her lifetime. A person of the earth, I suppose.

After today, I wasn't sure if this would be the last time I would see Emily. I had so many questions to which I needed answers. I couldn't stay silent any longer. I was part of this strange world, as well as their beliefs.

"How is it possible that a spirit could take over your body?" I questioned.

"Only in a weak state," Emily corrected, "in the same manner that your own spirit leaves your body in death. I guess it's a means of survival. Our spirit will always live on. Nék ne:'eh shonkwaya'tíhsonh (Only the Creator) can take that away."

When your senses are down through sickness or in an intoxicated state, most likely you wouldn't even know. Although it isn't unheard of, we know through our generations it has happened. A kanikonraksens (a dark spirit) can inhabit the human body, causing a sickness inside of them. Sometimes, it will take several ceremonies to get rid of the dark spirit. Unlike the shape shifters when they waken, only part of their spirit was human. Their spirits would never be whole again. They couldn't live without the spirit of the animal they had possessed.

"Was that the reason they had to go back to the willow each day?" Beth questioned.

Emily nodded her head in agreement. "Their spirits are still, when they are beside each other. The human side we were told was unsettled at first. After their death, they couldn't connect with their bodies. Né ne rotiksten'okónha' (The Old Ones) would tell of nightmarish screams following their burial. Over time they accepted what had to be. They will forever lie beside the bones and spirits of the animals they once possessed.

They are at sleep now, thanks to the Old One that still watches over our people. But I must tell you, it's not just respect that we avoided walking on their burial ground. We don't want to wake them, not even a stir.

One night when the ground hadn't quite thawed a small herd of deer began to move. You could hear the sound of hoofs clipping along against the hard ground a half-mile away. They crossed over the burial ground that night, wakening the spirits of the shape shifters. Ne' ó:nen kawera' shatsthe i:ken'neh (When there a strong wind it is) the most eerie sound as the wind carries their cries throughout the branches.

Our ancestors tried to discourage the herd from taking this path by dragging the dead roots and branches from the trees that had fallen from that area. In time the makeshift fence would rot away.

Repairs were made numerous times through the generations. We have often wondered what would draw the deer to this area. Many times they have found marks along the fence as if they were trying to knock it down with their hoofs. And it's not just the deer that seem to have an interest in the graves. Né rotiksten'o kón ha (The Old Ones) would tell stories of dogs being attracted to the far end of the willows. Many times, the roots were exposed as dogs continued to dig, as if they could smell the rancid smell of these bodies."

"But it has been hundreds of years since their bones were burned to ashes," Emily added as she poked at the charred remains of a branch just inside the fire.

"In the years that have followed, many daring men have since covered these holes and planted cedar trees where they could, trying to mask the odour that only dogs can smell. But deep inside we all knew the shape shifters would never be settled. They will always be waiting for that day to return, more so after what has happened," Emily said as her dark eyes met mine.

For a long moment, I too sat staring into the fire lost in my own thoughts, while the form of a small log slowly crumbled leaving only a pile of ash. Again, an unnerving feeling fell over me as I recalled standing beside Emily that night. Before long my mind drifted back to those same willows and that uneasy feeling that my very soul was being pulled from me, from far beneath the willows. I shuddered inside as I realized how close I had been to becoming one of them. I was blind to this world and to their beliefs, but had sincerely agreed to help Isaac in his need.

It was at that same instant, I could hear Emily's voice amongst my thoughts.

"When the Dark Spirit stepped into our world, he found he could control the shape shifters. They could live in this world again. Guided by this Dark Spirit, they hunted the weak unbeknownst to our people. This Dark Spirit could sense a weakness when a person was ill or under the influence of alcohol né tekahnikonráten:yes' (the mind changer). It was in this weak state, that some of the men that survived said they could feel a presence as if someone was standing near them. What little strength they had seemed to be drawn away, and within seconds the spirit of the shape shifter was living within them.

They couldn't stop what was happening to them. They complained to their families when they arrived home of not feeling well. Their thoughts were confused like they were in a heavy fog that wouldn't go away. They would start one conversation and end with another. As the days passed, their voices were no longer understood.

These spirits, as we have learned, can live inside one's body without their families knowing, but if they stay too long the human body ceases to survive. It was when one of the men crawled out from beneath the willows, he told of a nightmarish night. He remembered waking up in a panic as the smell of freshly turned soil filled the air around him. The odd thing, he remembered, was having the feeling there was someone lying next to him. He stretched out his arms in the darkness, but there was no one there. Still this uneasy feeling of movement stirred his greatest fear, being trapped beneath the willows.

It was in these moments he heard several low groans. At first, he laid motionless unsure of how he even came to be there. He could feel his heart racing as he realized he was right where he never wanted to be. But it was with his certainty of his culture and his belief he knew they couldn't rise, the shape shifters were bound. What happened next brought a chill to his bones. Something was slowly crawling over him, but it had no physical form?

Again he hears several groan. Scrambling to find the men, he pulled his way through the tangled roots. There he released the men that were imprisoned there. Still there were men left behind, it was too late for them. Guided by a glimmer of light from the morning sun, they had found a small opening. An opening only the dogs could have made. The men had no memory of how they got there, their joints swollen so bad they could barely walk.

We all had heard the stories that were circling around when it first started. It came on slowly at first. It appeared some of our men had some kind of break down, their thoughts seemed scrambled, like when you have a high fever.

"When I heard the men had gone missing," Emily continued, "I wasn't too concerned. I knew most of them and their families. It wasn't unusual for them to go hunting for weeks at a time. Still there were others that just couldn't stay away from the bottle. They couldn't see their despair had always been jarred up in that damn bottle. At the time, I had no doubt they would eventually wander home."

Emily shook her head with an awkward grin as sorrow seem to pull at an old memory.

"The stories had settled down after a while and I didn't think much about it. I guess I chose to believe it wasn't real, up until I met the Stranger myself. I felt safe in my community and besides, who would harm an old woman."

Emily's bottom lip protruded out and her face soured for a moment as she recalls that night standing within the willows. She laughs flippantly as she makes light of how close she was to death.

"Hmm!" a sound uttered from her mouth as anger pulls at her.

Her mind quickly pulled her back to that late afternoon when a truck pulled up beside her.

"I could see his grey hair peeking out from the rim of his hat. His nose was long and distorted. I opened the truck door to find a much younger man. His looks were striking. His voice pulled you near him. Believing my eyes were playing tricks on me because of the long day I had just spent, I climbed into the truck. His clothes seemed tidy, but nek tsi iken'ne a:se onhwentsyakarhatho wa'on téhswa'te (he smelled of freshly turned earth) like the soil that was freshly turned over. Before I realized what I had done it was too late," Emily said as she proceeded to pull back the sleeves of her jacket, showing the discolorations on the lower parts of her arms. "I couldn't get away. I felt the evil that was housed in this young man's body. The fear was unbearable."

Emily turned to Beth. "You know how you feel when you cross paths with someone you just don't like. It's that same feeling but a hundred times greater. I couldn't block the strength of the evil that was housed inside of him. A sick and helpless feeling threatened my sanity. Through my fear, and my sight that he had taken from me, I stayed silent. When the sounds of the night returned, I felt safe. They were all gone, but for how long I didn't know. I could feel my heart racing as I stumbled through the woods trying to find my way back out of this now unfamiliar land. Through my blindness I found this fire pit. I wasn't even sure what campsite I was in, not till the next morning when the sun's rays fell against the left side of my face, that and the two logs I found, not far from the fire pit."

"You couldn't imagine how frightened and confused I was the night that you came into the campsite. At first, I thought you were a part of what I had just gone through. The missing men, the willows, and the stranger, I put it all together. It could only mean one thing - the shape shifters had been wakened."

Emily slowly lowered her head as her hands fell against her face. "All my life, I have heard these stories. I always hoped that day would never come."

The Passing

"As a young girl, I didn't quite understand the stories of the willows or the concept of spirits being trapped beneath the ground. I only knew when you die your soul travels on to the spirit world. It wasn't until rakhsótha' (my grandfather) was quite ill, around the time of his death, that I witnessed something very strange," Emily said.

"I was in my early twenties and had lived with my grandfather most of my young life, along with khe'kén-ha' (my youngest sister). I realized then just how close we are to that other existence. It was my belief that a person has already died a year ahead of his time, so to speak, whether they're conscious of it or not. He or she feels a great urgency to finish things at hand, or to see loved ones they haven't seen for some time. Their need is so strong they materialize in other locations sometimes miles away."

"About a month before grandfather had passed away, he began to go missing, sometimes for minutes, sometimes longer. On several occasions I witnessed this. At first, I thought I must have been lost in my thoughts when I entered the empty room, walking right past grandfather's favourite chair. He wasn't there. When I turned to leave, he was sitting staring into the wall."

"Another time I saw him through the kitchen window sitting under a lean-to. He loved sitting out there in the midmorning. The warmth of the sun, he believed would heal his ailing joints. My sister, on that same morning, was coming up the pathway. She claims she saw him walking around the yard with a garden hoe, chopping those thick blue devils that littered our yard. The strangest part was she couldn't hear the footsteps of those old floppy brown steel-toed shoes he used to wear. She believed, shonkwah-sótha' ohsì:ta' kèn:ne ratkwitha néh ohonteh (grandfather's feet was moving over the grass) his feet never touched the ground," Emily said.

And for a moment, Beth saw a younger childlike side of Emily as her face softened. And for a long moment Emily lets her mind travel back, finding that day, seizing the image of her dear grandfather sitting under that old lean-to.

"I waved to him that day through the kitchen window and was about to place káksa'(a dish) on tsi ohswèn:kareh atekhwàrathserakayon (that old plank table) grandfather had made. It was here that I heard movement in his room. He was sitting up in his bed, his eyes were the darkest I have ever seen them. His hand was extending out as if he was talking to someone. I believe he was talking to the Old Ones, being prepared for his final journey," Emily said as she caught herself massaging her right wrist aggressively.

"Sorry! I guess I'm a lot like rakhsótha' (my grandfather). My achy joints only act up when the weather is about to change," Emily said as she turned away from me, as if she felt shame for revealing a small part of herself. Her long life I was slowly getting to know.

Emily gave a slight smile as she continued, "When grandfather's health was at its lowest, and his physical body was letting go, things began falling in the house after that time, small things as if they were tipped over. In the ending hour, things that shouldn't have fallen were lying on the floor. Some say it was our past relatives. They were letting us know they were here to guide him home. They won't leave his side."

"But it wasn't just things falling. There was movement in the house. You could feel it, as if someone was walking right past you. I tried to dismiss what I was feeling. It wasn't until I felt stillness inside me, like my heart was no longer beating in my chest. My feet could no longer move. I was afraid at first. I reached out clutching khe'kénha' o-néntsha' (my sister's arm) as she was about to step past me. In a whisper, I pleaded for her to stay with me. I can't seem to move."

Within seconds a soft glow of light seemed to be all around me. My sister describes the light entering the room as being the light from the morning sun as it passes through your window. It faded away just as quickly as it appeared. The Elders at that time believed a spirit had passed through me whether it was the spirit of grandfather or not, it may have tried to cling to my soul. So you see, one's spirit can leave his or her body, so why is it not believable that a Dark Spirit from another world can do the same.

"It's with this belief that we believe one of our hunters had leaped into the Stranger's world some hundred years ago, to retrieve his brother's soul. For if he didn't believe one's spirit could leave one's body he wouldn't have thought it was possible," Emily said as she pushed aside the high weeds and underbrush, while looking for some sizable dead branches she could use for her fire.

Beth began to poke at the fire that was now showing a steady flame. Her thoughts were unsettled with all that she had known about the death of her own family members. Emily could see Beth was troubled with what she had said.

"I won't tell you any more if you are feeling uncomfortable," Emily said.

Emily quickly coaxed Beth to help gather more wood for the fire and at the same time she knew it would take her mind off things.

"I never much liked sleeping in the woods without a fire, more so with what has happened. There is something about the darkness. It's hard to separate what you're feeling. Is it real or is it all in your mind? This is where your gut feelings come into play," Emily said with a slight grin.

I nodded my head in agreement, telling Emily, "Maybe we should hold off on the stories till morning."

It was getting late and with the lack of sleep, I was finding myself slowly breaking away from the conversation. Still, I didn't want to offend her in any way. I quickly let her know.

"I still would like to hear more about the two brothers who were hunters, maybe on our walk home," I said, trying to sound more cheerful.

The soft pine branches weren't at all what Emily claimed they would be, but I slept waking periodically through the night, as thunder rumbled and lightening lit up the sky all around us.

That night I had the oddest dream. I dreamt I was standing in a field, but as I looked down at the ground it became dry and cracked. When I looked again, as far as my eyes could see, only black stumps remained where trees and houses once stood. In my dream, I fell back against the ground while an overwhelming feeling of dread filled my soul, and out of the darkened sky I saw a huge missile. Its force had rippled the sky, like I was lying under water. I watched as the missile passed over me missing the earth.

I could hear a voice. It seemed to be all around me. "When it comes around again, it will be too late."

When I woke I could barely move. I felt a sickness run through my body. I was there. I felt its fury. It was real.

"We all had a similar dream," the voice spoke again.

Hearing a sudden movement next to me, I turned to find Emily staring down at me while the morning light parted the trees behind her.

"Dreams are funny things. Sometimes they don't really say much, just trying to guide us, when we're having troubles," Emily said.

"The missile has appeared to many of our people in a dream. Quite a few of our seers have passed on or getting old. One thing they agree on, a change is coming. Whatever comes next, it will come with a force and the devastation will lie in the hands of the world. The charred remains of our forest bring a great warning to our people," Emily continued.

The source of our healing is rooted in the bed of the forest, even to walk or sit in the woods. It gives off a healing power, quietening our minds when we are troubled. Without that unity of plants and trees, that accord will cease. Conflict will stretch across our communities. I believe that the harmony in many places around the world has long ago left this world with the depleting of their forests, a world that is so often pulled apart in conflict.

With the great loss of trees in our own territory, we will start seeing a change. From the beginning of time, the forest has always protected us, whether it's to fuel our fires in the winter or to shelter us from the hot sun in the summer. We can only believe planting new trees will make our earth stronger and through the birds and animals our medicine will be plentiful.

"And it's not just the forest," Emily added. "Our clan mothers have pleaded with our young about the importance of our ceremonies and the loss of our beliefs. Where will they stand when that day comes. Our Elders will continue to watch for signs."

Close Connection

"There is one thing I do know about this forest," Emily chuckled, breaking the gloomy feeling we now felt hanging over us. "There is a creek nearby. More than likely there will be yoyentáthen (dry firewood) lying round after the creek had swollen over its banks last spring. And it will be a good gesture to leave some firewood for the next person."

Emily quickly kicked the charred remains of a small log back onto the fire pit while she assured me it wouldn't take long. It was just over the hill. I instantly felt its hold as I stood looking over a small ravine and I couldn't help but think that time had somehow stopped here. The dead branches that had fallen from the winter before had created a picture in my mind. Their long grey fingers seemed to be crawling along through the thick green foliage that lay along this forty foot incline. At the bottom of this ravine, a small creek laced through the young trees and shrubs as far as I could see.

And for a moment, I stood breathless, as my mind pulled at an old memory of walking with my father along the flats not far from our own home. It was the long green ferns that pulled at my memory even further. The ferns seemed to border along what few trees survived this once marshy basin. In that next instant, I thought how good it would have been to pick a basketful of fiddleheads. Yet, in that same instant, the oversize leaves told me they were already gone to seed.

Nothing seemed out of the ordinary in this picturesque place.

My thoughts quickly faded hearing the sounds of twigs snapping just over the hill. Emily and I cautiously turned from the bushes that we were combing through.

"Sounds like something is in the woods with us," I said in a low voice.

Emily snapped a dead branch easily under the heavy boots she was wearing. Then she hurried along picking up any small pieces of firewood she could, while she made her way back up the hill. And for a moment I could feel myself falling back letting Emily lead as caution pulled at my nerves.

Hearing the sound of small branches snapping, and the uneven footsteps of something rushing toward us had my heart racing. The only thing that came to mind was the large buck we had last seen near the two boulders. A sick feeling was now churning inside me as I anticipated the worst. Was I as much a fool as Emily was climbing into the stranger's truck? Did I really know this woman? My thoughts were rapid as I tried to block what I was thinking. I had always prided myself on making good judgment when it came to new people I just met. But this forest had an uncanny way of altering how I perceive things now. Things were not always what they appeared to be.

That faint sound I'd thought I heard as a child? There was no one there, nor were the shadows I thought I had seen. I was taught to dismiss these things. It's just the sound of the house settling. And for the shadows, sometimes your eyes play tricks on you, my mother would say.

Caution would now forever pull at my mind. My mind had been altered. Emily didn't seem alarmed and for a moment I considered if I should drop the small logs I was carrying and be prepared to defend myself. My feet froze in place as a sigh of relief escaped from my mouth. Isaac stepped out from the bushes just from over the hill. Following close behind were three other men. We both smiled, happy to see a familiar face.

"Shé:kon! (Hello!) I was wondering who would be coming to find me," Emily joked and gave her head a sight bow in a gesture of a thank you.

The taller man laughs and questions Emily, "Aren't there rules about walking in the woods," referring to the branch Emily had snapped under her boot.

"Yeah, keep a keen eye and walk lightly," Emily laughs, as she seems to know this man. "Besides that rule doesn't apply to me and how else would you find me," Emily said as she pushed aside a lower branch with her back.

I quickly stepped past her and found myself standing back at the same clearing. It was here that I watched as this taller man kneels down on one knee next to the fire pit and began to arrange the small pieces of firewood he picked up along the way.

"The one looking after the fire is ri'kénha' (my younger brother) Carter," Emily said.

With a concerned voice Carter turns to Emily, "sáta'karì:te ken?" (Are you well?) "Hén:enh waka-ta'karí:te," (Yes, I am well) Emily said. "We were worried about you. We heard a strange sound while searching the woods, like a loud wailing sigh as if it was ne rón:kwe' (a man) taking his last breath. But there was no one around."

Unnerving feeling ran up my back as this strange wailing sigh continued to circle the branches just above us. But what was even stranger, the sound didn't fade away as we would have thought. We were left frozen in our tracks as we listened to this strange mournful sigh continue to weave through trees in the distance. Whatever it was, we believed this man didn't just die. Raonha yehatonnhets ronenhsk-wenh (His soul was taken), wrenched from his body as if by unseen hands. When the sounds of the woods returned, we followed the only direction the sound could have come from, the willows.

A deep sigh escaped from Carter, as he turned to Emily, "We didn't want to believe what we were thinking. We are just glad you're safe."

For a long moment Beth and Emily were lost in their own thoughts as they relived those same mournful cries as Jim was swept into the underworld.

"The stranger won't be troubling anyone any more," Emily said as she broke the hush that seemed to be hanging over all of us.

Emily acknowledged Isaac for his insight and Beth her courage.

Isaac and the youngest of the four had made them-selves comfortable on the larger log on the opposite side of the fire. The husky man took a seat on a stump away from the others and began skinning the rabbits that were strung together with a twine. He quickly eased the rabbit's fur down the length of its body. That one there is my youngest brother Gilbert, Gil as he is most often called.

Emily waved her hand in Gil's direction, as he gave his head a sight bow.

"I'll rinse them off at the creek," Gil said and proud-ly raised his arms high as he showed off his kill. "There will be plenty for breakfast," he boasted.

An obvious place they must visit from time to time, I thought. I couldn't help thinking that Gil was rinsing the rabbits off in the creek for my sake. Otherwise, he'd put a skewer right through them after they were skinned. I gave a polite smile.

Emily made a crooked smiled as she introduced the youngest of the group. "This is my nephew Silas, the new buck," Emily said as she pointed to the younger man sitting on a log.

"Ohnìiohtonhátie?" (How's it going along) Silas said with a grin.

I raised my head and gave a pleasant, "Hello."

"A stone fed inside the ears of a burlap bag makes a perfect catch to tie the twine around," Silas said, and gave the braided twine that was still harnessed over his shoulders a tug.

An old thermos was pulled from the burlap sack. Silas snickered as Beth stared blankly at the thermos. Carter and Gil joined in the laughter as they caught his meaning.

"Nahò:ten' (What!) I found it just inside the boundary line," Silas laughingly said.

For some time Beth said nothing. "You can have it," Beth smiled while remembering she had mistakenly left her pack on the ground while she tied a kerchief around a tree marking her entry.

Gil reaches over at this point and gives Silas a nudge as he sits down beside him. "He has lots to learn," Gilbert said, referring to the knapsack he showed his nephew how to make.

They both laughed rowdily. Gil quickly challenges a strength contest between the two by throwing his arm outward directly across Silas's chest, knocking him back as he strains to remain on the log.

Silas reaches out grabbing Gilbert's collar just long enough to gain his balance. With his left arm he takes his uncle Gilbert down with a chokehold. Beth could see they were closer in age and must hassle each other from time to time.

"We took a chance coming out here," Carter said, referring to the willows, all the while ignoring his brother and nephew as they brush the dirt and leaves from their clothes.

"We were seeing some strange things in this part of the woods in the last couple of days," Carter went on saying.

"We must have seen a hundred or more apparitions, some at times moving right along side us, some looked to be going into battle. Some you would swear they were live. The Old Ones had returned, and they weren't just our Kanyen'kehaka (Mohawk) people, other clans had come through banding together as one Nation. There was onenyotehàka (Oneida), onontakehàka (Onondaga), kayonkwehaka (Cayuga), shotinontowane'haka (Seneca) and the tahkaró:ka (Tuscarora). They would materialize, and then fade away, only to reappear in another location. We kept our distance as we followed, but it was the direction they were heading that pulled at our nerves, "shape shifters." Words even now seem to leave an uneasy look on Carter's face."

"It's been a long time since anything like this has happened in our territory," Carter said as he looked around catching the eyes of Emily as he was still looking for answers from her.

"A memory so clear," Beth began to tremble as Emily recreates what took place, as the sun's light pierces between the two boulders.

It was also here in my thoughts that I realized the strength I had come to know after my marriage ended, was nothing compared to what strength I was desperately trying to hold onto, as I braved the last couple of days. Emily also seemed to let go of some of her strength. This toughness, I felt, had always protected her mentally and physically. I listened, as her voice seems to soften just a little in the comfort of her family as she continued.

"Né ne rotiksten'okónha (The Old Ones) fought a great battle," Emily began as she takes us back. "Overwhelmed with fear, we watched as the ghostly beings of the underworld pushed up through the opening we were trying to seal. Our very souls began to tremble as fear devoured any strength we had. It was here we believed our fate was near. But in the next instant, my heart rejoiced as we watched the Old Ones take to the sky. Their translucent bodies now began to take on a physical form of their once former bodies. Hundreds of warriors appeared in the sky with their war clubs and bows. It was at that same moment I caught something moving along the opposite cliff. The markers were toppling over from that old burial ground. You couldn't imagine the relief I felt when I saw them take to the sky and join the Old Ones in battle."

"The fear I once felt as a child, shaken as the older children told stories of the haunted burial ground. It was real and it wasn't just seeing misty figures moving alongside the markers from time to time, as was told when I was a child. Some of their translucent bodies were also lifelike."

I watched the faces of Carter and Gilbert, as well as Isaac, as their shoulders broadened just a little, proud of their heritage. They seemed to know what took place, as their smiles seem to hold their own memory. In their mind's eye, they could almost see the faces of the Old Ones as they take to the sky forcing the dark spirits of the underworld back down into its depth. And for a long moment more, they could almost feel the strength they once felt as their fathers and grandfathers told of the Old Ones pledge to watch over our people.

Hear our voices and know that our voices speak the truth when you hear our whisper forewarning you of danger.

Listen not for our invisible footsteps, for we walk among you in battle. And know that the Old Ones will guide you, when your steps falter.

Stand tall on-kwe-hón:weh (Native people) and bravery will continue in life.

Story of the Two Brothers

Emily encourages Isaac to tell the story of the two brothers while the rabbits slowly cooked over the fire.

"This is where the story I've been waiting to tell you about gets interesting, brings it to life so to speak." Emily said with a half grin.

Isaac slowly raises his head, his hands still cupped together between his knees. He turns, catching that glimpse of approval in Emily's eyes as he begins. He next looks directly at Silas and then at myself catching our attention.

"Isaac always liked to impact the young with the history and beliefs of our people, so the stories are never forgotten," Emily whispers.

"Whether you believe in the spiritual world or not, you must listen with an open mind," Isaac began. "Our great-grandfathers would tell of a story that to some was unbelievable. Some of our people had the power to cross over to another existence and still return. This man Emily was referring to was a great warrior, a fearless man," Isaac said proudly.

"It has been over two hundred years. The two brothers I'll name Joe and Henry," Isaac said as he glanced at

Beth. "They were returning home from a day of hunting, when Joe felt his younger brother Henry drop his end of the long pole. Joe turned to scold Henry as ohskennón:tonh (deer) slid onto the ground."

"Something is here in the woods with us," Henry warned in a low whisper.

"Whatever it is, it's moving real fast," Joe warns.

Joe cautions his younger brother by nudging him in the arm and points to a line of young trees. They were slumped over halfway up as if they were pushed by a strong wind. Unaware of the danger lurking behind them, Joe suddenly felt a force knocking him to the ground. He turns back in disbelief as a dark mist seized his younger brother. He watches as his brother's still body slips to the ground.

It was in this moment, he saw what was beyond belief. His brother's spirit was being pulled from his body. Joe's will was strong that day. Enraged, Joe leaped forward seizing his brother's spirit. Within seconds the void was closed. To his surprise, he was also pulled into this strange world. He watches as Henry's spirit is tossed to the ground only to roll into a glowing ball of light. Joe's rage burns even stronger as he watches Henry's spirit swiftly being pulled through the darkness at a speed he couldn't possibly match.

In his rage, he knows he must take control if he wants to ever see his brother again. But it is that rage that fuels his ability to travel through this portal, for no man could ever survive this cold dark world. Only the most evil of men are believed to be there. Their tortured souls cry out as creatures of this underworld pull them down even farther into its fiery depth.

Joe continued to follow these creatures with no concern for himself. It's here in the darkness he could hear Henry's screams echoing throughout the tunnels. He soon realizes he was being lured down farther into its depth. One by one the hideous faces lunge toward him as he struggles to keep his sanity. Fearing all hope is about to be lost, Joe's rage fuels a power so strong he tosses the demons from the grip that they now have on him.

"My brother doesn't belong here," Joe shouts.

In his rage he demands they release him. Suddenly, an unknown grip has a hold of him. This beast seems almost human as it towers over the other creatures. His body is covered with long reddish brown hair from his head down to his huge feet. He lets out a scream that sounded almost like a loud moan, in a dialect only the creatures could understand.

Joe was now being dragged in the opposite direction along with his younger brother's spirit. In an instant, Joe and Henry were swept back into our world. The brothers watch in disbelief as the creature's long stride quickly bound him down the steep gully. His lengthy legs quickly moved him along the creek, as the forest seemed to blend around him.

They say it was the last time the two brothers ever saw this longhaired creature. The strange part to this story is, when Joe and Henry woke, three days had since passed. They were found exhausted, plagued with the haunted memories of hideous faces and the sound of mournful cries. As weeks passed, the oddest things began to happen, their joints began to swell, their bodies slowly began to curve - a curse that has afflicted their families ever since.

It was also at that moment in time that the Dark Spirit (the Stranger) had witnessed the passage between the two worlds. This kanikonraksen (Dark Spirit) hid in the shadows and watched as a sliver of light so bright pierced the darkness, blinded all that followed. As it was, more than two hundred years have since passed.

When a young man named Jim, wrongfully removed the protection that surrounds our territory, not sure of his words, the portal to the underworld was once again open. The Dark Spirit was free to exist in our world.

This Dark Spirit hid among our people, learning our ways. It was here that it learned of the shape shifters buried within the roots of the willows. Once released, the Dark Spirit took control. He watched as their human spirits leap into the bodies of the animals in a nearby woods. In an instant, their new body sprang to life. They were faster, stronger and were able to see farther.

Without any hesitation, the Dark Spirit stepped into a large buck. This Dark Spirit was now living and breathing in our world. He could be any animal he wanted to be. But what intrigued the Dark Spirit even more was the tall man cloaked in black, a Stranger just passing through. He watches as this man pulls his truck over, along a back road. The Dark Spirit could see his strength as he lifted the spare tire with ease.

Without any warning, the Dark Spirit became that man. This Stranger was now being sighted in our territory, but never near enough to see his true form. The Dark Spirit could now travel anywhere he wanted, free to travel beyond our territory. He now had the power he had waited for.

Once under the Stranger's control, the shape shifters not only could become animal or bird, they had the power to transfer their spirit into human bodies, although for only a short time. It satisfied the Stranger's needs. One by one his order was filled as the shape shifters stepped into the unmindful humans. In time, he could release his kind from their hellish existence, a soul for a soul.

Silas nervously skimmed over the treetops and low bushes looking for the slightest movement. He recalls the terror he once felt when he first became aware of what had happened. The shape shifters had been awakened. He anxiously asked Isaac if the Dark Spirit was gone for good.

Isaac's mind quickly pulls at everything they had done when preparing the ceremony. A ceremony he had fulfilled in his frail condition after a dog attack. It was set in place to coincide with Beth as she closed the void to the underworld.

"I believe so, whatever spirit that came from the underworld was driven back down with the Dark Spirit. Our people who survived will heal. Their families will be by their side till their flu symptoms disappear."

Far From the Stars We See

"What troubles me more is what else came through the day Jim removed the protection from our territory? Maybe not from the underworld, but far from the stars we see. That shield that protects the earth, once that shield is open, even a sliver of light can invite the unwelcome," Isaac warns.

'We can only hope nothing else had come through that day," Isaac said.

"That could explain some things that were bothering me," Gilbert said. "I had been fishing along the river a few weeks ago, when I spotted an elderly man sitting along the bank. He looked out of character as the elderly man was wearing a brown suit. He never spoke other than a few grunts when I asked if the fish was running. I stayed about an hour and then decided to change my place along the river. The old man didn't move from where he was sitting."

"Finding a favourite spot, I settled in. Within seconds from throwing my line in, the old man was sitting next to me. A vision now appeared before me. This is also strange because I have never had a vision in my life. In my vision, I could see a barefoot man walking toward me in an open meadow. A strange fog seemed to be rolling behind him. His oval shaped eyes were as black as coal, not like the light eyes of the old man who sat next to me. His fingers and bare toes seemed longer than most people and some of his toes were fused together. When the vision ended, I turned to find the old man was nowhere in sight. An unnerving feeling fell over me as I stood and watched a mysterious mist trail the path along the river. Whatever I saw, I don't believe he was from this world."

Isaac seemed lost in his thoughts for a moment.

"I do know of a story that has troubled our people in the past. At that moment Isaac's head slightly tilted to the side, nék tsi wahonnise'kenha eh ni tyawen:onh (but it happened a long time ago). As a young boy, my father and my three brothers would often visit our grandfather making sure he wasn't in need of anything. We came so often a path was made through the woods. Grandfather was a tolerant man and would wait patiently for the horseplay to settle down. We anxiously pushed our way through the doorway to behold a museum of antlers and old o'tá:ra' kanàtsyonk (clay pots). Each was filled with a collection of arrowheads, clay pipes and metal buttons.

"I can tell you what each arrowhead was made for," grandfather chuckled as he shifted the large piece of buckskin that was draped over an oversized bench.

And as always he challenged us into making our own ahtahkwa'ón:weh (moccasins). Our father had agreed as we turned up the sole of our shoes. The laughter had settled by this time and with grandfather's last cut, he held up a large piece of buckskin against the ohnénhsa:ke shonkwa'níha (shoulders of our father). A jacket rakeniha (my father) would treasure for years.

As it was in the past, it wasn't long before grandfather would begin to tell stories passed down from his father, stories he had told many times before, but with respect we said nothing.

But this night was different. An old friend of grand-father's had come to visit days earlier. He warned grand-father that something strange was going on in our terri-tory. He was one of the dozen people that could see spirits, along with my grandfather. He warned these spirits have a strange look to them, long distorted faces.

"We don't hear of these spirits as often any more and if we do we don't make eye contact with them, most of the time they just fade away," Isaac said.

"And if you do make eye contact?" Beth ques-tioned.

"They step through. You don't want to ever take that chance," Isaac warned.

"They cling to your soul controlling your thoughts. When the shape shifters were wakened, we did question our beliefs at that time, if we were hearing similar stories from our past. But they're not the same. These creatures do materialize, although we don't believe these creatures can live in our world for any length of time. We believe there is a mist, a shield that covers who they are."

"Many of our hunters at that time said they could feel a presence moving alongside them as they walked through the woods. They kept their eyes lowered, their bodies still until they had passed. The odd thing was there was a strange mist that seemed to trail close behind these strange auras," Isaac said.

Don't Walk on the Road
After Dark

"As a young man it was hard to believe these stories that were passed down were real," Carter said. "It wasn't until one night that my belief changed. My cousin Horace and I were out one night when we were about eighteen years of age. In those days you couldn't tell us anything. Horace was towering, tallest guy I ever knew. His father used to say he was as big as a barn, a tough son of a b…. Carter stops as he caught Beth's eyes."

"He was as tough as nails and he boasted every chance he got," Carter laughingly said as he watched for Beth's expression to change.

Silas laughed out loud and quickly scratched the back of his head blushing as he caught Carter glance in Beth's direction. There was one thing about Silas that his family didn't know - he was good at reading people. Being a very passive child, he was often bullied. Silas began to develop awareness when he was around these children. It was as if he could feel their emotions almost to a point where he believed he knew what they were going to say next.

Silas looked around at his uncles. It was different with his uncle Gilbert. They grew up more like brothers, teasing and laughing with each other as long as he could remember. His uncle Carter was more like his father, he couldn't hear their thoughts their kindness prevented it.

Something had changed in his uncle, the moment he met Beth. It was something in Carter's eyes that had softened. Carter liked Beth. Beth's head slightly turned as if she knew Carter was looking at her.

"Did they share the same feelings?" Silas thought.

His uncle was still a good-looking man and lived alone much longer than most. Silas silently wished this uncle the best. Silas quickly pulled away from his thoughts as he could hear Carter talking about a lacrosse game.

"We were attending attsihkwá:'eh (a lacrosse game) that was held at the Ononta'kehà:kah kanónhsehs (Onondaga Longhouse) and had stayed much longer then we should have. Walking on foot, we decided we would catch up with his friend Carl along the way. Maybe have a few drinks at his home, about a half a mile outside our territory. His friend was somewhat older, maybe early twenties. We never asked, but Horace seem to be pretty good friends with him and Carl always had a bottle of wine hidden under the floorboard just inside the barn. I supposed that was why Horace was the way he was. It was some time later that I learned Carl's dad was a bootlegger. We figure he just continued after his father had died.

Carter slightly turned his head and for a moment he remembered the recklessness of their youth.

"It was in those days that the law would patrol the outskirts of our territory. Sometimes we would hear stories of men spending thirty days in jail for drinking. We both laughed knowing we would probably know someone in there, being our people were picked up many times for walking across the road the wrong way. We laughed again that night when the question was brought up where we would meet if we had to run. In those days, the officials had been ordered to pick up truants, but mostly they went around picking up anyone who looked to be intoxicated. And if our people were off our territory it meant you were probably up to something, so they thought. Officials believed our people couldn't tolerate alcohol. Maybe so, the clan mothers had agreed, saying it was like a poison to our mind."

"Scaring the daylights out of some of the government officials," Carter said with a half grin.

"Still there were times when our young men were just knocked around and let go. You wouldn't dare raise your hand. Being locked up for thirty days didn't appeal to any of us."

But there was something about the spring air that brought the fight out of Horace that day. Horace didn't have a care in the world. He boasted he was ready for a fight. We quickly raised our fists into the air as a long forgotten warrior's cry escaped from our mouths. Cries that still echo in the mind of our age-old grandfathers as they watched their fathers before them go into battle.

I knew it was a bad idea when I stepped onto the road that night especially after we had been drinking, more so for Horace, but he was bent on having that next drink. It wasn't long before the sky grew dark. And it was only then that we felt the road seemed longer than usual. Horace began complaining about his hard sole shoes, like they were made of stone he had said. I could also feel the weight, that and the blister that was forming along the back of my foot. Still I encouraged Horace to keep moving.

"We don't have far to go. We will be at your friend's house in no time. It will be okay," Carter said.

Horace knew what Carter meant. Their families had often spoke of these back roads, hearing strange sounds and seeing some odd lights going at a high speed, some flying right past their heads not more than ten feet away.

"Katehswà:-tha (I smell something). What is that awful smell?" Horace said.

I could see the outline of Horace in the darkness as he was pulling his shirt up to cover his nose. We finally agreed the smell was coming from a swamp about couple of miles away in the opposite direction. It was a trail our ancestor had named Sour Springs, although we never thought the smell could reach this far. Still it satisfied our worst fear that we had somehow taken the wrong road and we would have to pass the old burial ground. The burial ground scared us more than the odd lights.

Finally, after watching Horace stumbling along, we both agreed to sit and rest for awhile just inside the shallow ditch that stood in front of us. When it was time to leave Horace refused, saying he just needed to rest longer. After several attempts to keep him awake, I finally agreed to let Horace sleep longer knowing he had pretty much drank most of the day. I had no fear he couldn't handle himself if he had to, so I left him behind.

It was becoming a strange night walking alone with the sound of twigs snapping periodically around me, more so when a dense fog came creeping across the open meadow and that awful smell still lingering in the air.

I must have walked about a mile or more in the dense fog, all the while trying to stay along the edge of the road. The strange part was when I began recalling the stories I'd heard as a child, things our Elders saw and heard and even felt while walking after dark. Not just sounds of animals, but sounds of voices that couldn't be described as human. And there were other sounds, like the stride of footsteps a man would make, but as always there was never anyone there.

Before long my mind began playing tricks on me. I too could almost hear the distant sound of a wagon as the story unfolded in my mind, a man being run over struck by a horse and wagon. The more I thought about it the more I found myself wanting to know, how was that possible? A horse wouldn't just run over a man. You would at least hear the horse's footsteps in the darkness, giving you enough time to get out of the way. What would make a man run his horse in the dense fog like that? Unanswered questions kept going through my mind.

Still it wasn't unusual, I told myself, for people returning from town in the late hours hauling their goods home. Some of the farmers from neighbouring communities would come along the outskirts of our territory selling liquor to our people and a wagon of hay was a perfect cover.

My thoughts quickly faded. I could hear that same sound of hoofs stepping along at a slow pace and the distinctive sound of an uneven cartwheel close behind. Within minutes, a man pulled up alongside me. Although I couldn't make out his face, his voice made me think that he was somewhat old. Trembling inside at the eerie feeling that seemed to be filling around me, I quickly told myself, "It's just roksténha (an old man)."

I immediately asked, "How is it that you and your horse can see through this fog?"

"This old mare knows every inch of this road. We travel through this way every night about this time," the old man said. His voice was deep and coarse, but yet there was an even tone to it.

I asked if he had seen my cousin, describing his weight and height. "You couldn't miss him," I told the old man.

"I'm going back that way, just dropping some goods off at the next farmhouse and if you get in I'll help you find him," the old man offered.

It was here that same eerie feeling seemed to now be weighing heavy over my thoughts. There was no farmhouse along this stretch of road. It was in this moment that I caught the sound of footsteps shuffling along the road behind me.

"Did you hear that sound?" I whispered.

"The night carries a lot of sounds. It's best we keep moving," the old man said.

When I turned back, the old man was gone. The strange part was, I never heard a sound from that rutted cartwheel again or that awful sour smell that had remained in the air.

I immediately called out to Horace several times believing he had changed his mind and I wouldn't have to walk alone. There was never an answer. Frightened of what else was in the dark, I ran, stopping and resting along the way whenever there was a clearing in the fog.

Horace never came home that night. But family and friends claim to have seen him in the early morning just before sunrise, always along the same road where he was last seen. His clothes were tattered, and his facial features were distorted with dark shadows. Whatever it was, something evil was in the dark that night.

Carter's head slightly turned from the others as he fights with the sorrow he once felt.

Horace

What people don't know is that Horace did wake that night not long after Carter had left. Horace could have sworn someone was pulling at his feet, first one then the other. Annoyed, he kicked out his lengthy legs and heard a distinct sound of something fall firmly in the ditch. He did try calling out Carter's name while accusing him of messing with his shoes before he remembered Carter saying he was leaving and would meet at his friend's house. He laughed out loud as he scrambled to his feet.

"Yah tehonkwe'tawa:nen enhakwaya'tayentáne," (There's not a man big enough to take me down), he shouted as he stepped up onto the road. He was right. There wasn't one man who could take him down.

Horace strained to see what was in the darkness the best he could, but there was nothing he could not identify as unusual, just a light mist floating along the length of the ditch he had moments ago stepped out from. Horace watched and waited a little longer someone or something was near. He could feel it. Blinking several times he questioned the fog as it pulled itself closer. Then the most unusual shape began to emerge from the fog. Its serpent-like head seemed to rise, as it appeared to be looking directly at Horace. Horace found himself stepping back and for a moment he awkwardly laughed at the silliness he was thinking. Still, he didn't heed the warning and the ill feeling he felt in his stomach.

"It's just the fog," Horace said out loud.

More so, so he could hear himself and tried to convince himself there was nothing odd about this fog. He watched as the mist is now pulling itself in his direction. Its lengthy body slowly began to coil around his feet. He could now feel the buckskin of his jacket tighten around him as the fog begins to consume his upper body.

Still Horace stands in disbelief as he feels stillness inside of his body like his heart was no longer beating. For a moment he compares his hazy thoughts with drinking too much that day. It was only when he felt his throat tighten that Horace pulled away from his trance-like state and wa'tharáhtate akwah ken niyohsnore tsi wahokweni (he ran just as fast as he could).

What feels like only minutes, the distance he has run wrenches in his chest. His mind is only on one thing now. He leans forward as his hands clutch his knees. Slowly, he takes the next agonizing breath. Slowly and calmly he exhales as he feels the pain in his chest subside. Again he tries to make sense of what had just happened.

He tells himself, a-kwah ne:e' tyotsha'a yeńthonh (it's only the mist).

But his culture has taught him something different. Stories pass down for generations. There must be some truth to them.

"Sewatyé:renh ronón-ha' i:hon:ne tsi niwahson:tehs." (Sometimes they walk during the night).

These words kept going through his mind. Horace stands partly stooped over. His hands are more out of his pocket than they are in. And through all that has happened he thinks about his weight. I can't even put my hands in my pockets. I can't even run to save myself.

Horace stood looking out into the darkness. Slowly his head lowers as he stares down at the darkness in front of his feet. Whether he believed in prayer or not he felt a great urgency to speak to shonkwaya'tíh-sonh (the Creator). He stood in silence and for a long moment the whole being of his soul pulls to the heavens as he fights for the answer he needs. Without another thought, he vows he will stand and fight with whatever comes tonight.

Horace's bottom lip protrudes outward as he stands looking out over a small hill he is now standing on, his eyes straining to see what lies at the foot of the hill. About five hundred feet away, he is certain he will find the rusted railing of the old bridge. A bridge he will have to cross. He tucks his long hair in his collar as he prepares himself. Nihononkweta:a nihonna:sa (Little People), some say they live under the bridges, stand about a foot high or more. No one has ever seen them up close, but they swear they have seen them darting away between the underbrush and the high weeds. But it wouldn't be the Little People circling around him that he should fear.

Out over the creek, came a much heavier fog. Horace watches as the fog pulled itself up out of the water while slowly consuming the bridge. It's here in the fog that Horace hears small voices telling him to run. Again he stops as he tries to make sense of what is going on.

Slowly and certain he watches as a man steps out from the fog. Although he can't make out the man's features, he can see his head was oddly shaped. His nose and jaw seem to protrude outward.

Horace stood tall as he flexed his shoulders. His large hands soon rolled into a fist as he anticipates a fight. At the same time, he hears the rustling of small feet as they charge ahead of him with metal objects and sticks. Horace watched as this man falls to the ground. For a moment the fog seems to retract as it cowers away, but in a blink of an eye a ghostly figure stands in front of him. Horace feels his chest tighten as he draws in his last breath.

"Are you saying the man's spirit had entered Horace's body that night?" Beth questioned.

"I don't think kí:ken atonn-hets ne ron:kwe (this soul was of a man). Whatever it was, it had masked itself inside this old man's body," Carter said. "When daylight came, the body of the old man was found slumped against the railing of the bridge. His horse was discovered half a mile away still attached to its cart."

When authorities came out, a few of our people hid in the bushes. Out of curiosity they watched and listened. They heard the authorities say that when they picked up the old man his legs seemed to rattle as if his bones were in pieces. The skin along his jawbone seemed to hang as if he had lost a great amount of weight.

"It was a strange time in those days," Carter said as he stares at the ground in front of him. For a long moment, Carter tried to hang on to his cousin's memory, a glimpse of an old friend in better times. It was in that instant, that Beth sees Carter's shoulders slump forward, while his strength seems to fall around him. Although it was a long time ago, we all felt Carter's sorrow at that moment as silence fell over us.

Isaac Gives Warning

"I have been questioning my own thoughts, if these are the same beings I saw as a young boy," Isaac spoke up. "They travel from other worlds far beyond the stars we see," Isaac said as he glanced in Beth and Silas's direction catching their eyes with his.

They were the newcomers. Carter and Gil, as well as Emily, knew what Isaac was implying. They all gave their heads a slight bow as Isaac continued.

"I first became aware of these beings when I was about fourteen and had seen them only twice in my life as I made my way to the river. The first time, I thought I was looking at my father's brother. He was a large man. His shoulders were wide and bulky, like he could lift a tree," Isaac said with a slight smile. "He was at a shouting distance from where I was walking. I was about to call out to him when I noticed he appeared to be searching for something in the high grass. He immediately pulled out his knife and began frantically running through the high weeds."

"It was at that moment I saw ónyareh onón:tsi (a snake head) rise up over the high grass. It was larger than any snake I ever saw. What was odd, I could have sworn this serpent was running on four legs. In the next instant a white mist appeared. Within seconds it floated directly above rakenohá:ah (my uncle). In disbelief, I watched as my uncle was drawn up into the white mist, while another dark mist followed. As a young boy, I was so frightened I fell to the ground and hid among the high weeds believing my uncle wasn't all what I thought he was, a witch of sort. It wasn't until I saw the hopelessness on my uncle's face the second time that I understood.

Weeks had passed. Still my uncle hadn't returned and my curiosity was pulling at this unbelievable story I had witnessed. I could see family and friends were giving up, and it wasn't as if I had seen his death. Something had taken him.

For a brief moment my mind pulled at an old memory of sitting alongside my grandfather while the last embers fade into the darkness.

"Remember to always keep your wits about you. Your warnings will be there," my grandfather cautioned.

As an adolescent, I couldn't see the likelihood of any danger this apparition could bring upon me. It would be my stubbornness to find my uncle that would block the warning that would be given to me. Again, I felt compelled to find an answer. I let my curiosity lead me back into the woods. I hadn't walked more than a couple of hours when I spotted my uncle in a fortress of trees. I quickly found myself looking from behind a large bush, while caution now pulled at me from every direction.

The mist was nowhere in sight. Guessing all was well I rushed towards my uncle? Suddenly my vision became unclear, like I was seeing him through the bottom of a glass jar. He was trapped. I desperately smashed my fist against this unseen shield wanting to release him. It was only then I realized his eyes showed no emotions. His body was still. It was that same moment that a white mist began forming just behind him. The next instant my uncle was gone.

The dark mist that I had seen before now began to emerge from the ground. It had the intelligence to conceal itself. In one bound, it perched itself high onto a nearby tree. I could barely believe what my eyes were showing me. This dark mist could blend itself against the bark of the tree like the grey tree frog. *It could camouflage itself!* It did, while lying against the ground only inches from where I was standing behind the large shrub. Whatever these beings were, they had been watching me.

I found myself racing toward the tree, picking up any small rocks I could find. It was here in my battle to survive that I distinctly saw a definite shape forming in the mist. A protruding face and the bulk in its long arms and shoulder told me this entity was more of a lizard than a serpent. It could walk on all fours.

Seconds now turned to minutes as I came face to face with this creature. It was only then that I felt something in its eyes. It had a power over me. My knee fell beneath me, its eyes voiced I was not leaving. The rocks I had gripped in my hands now slid from my hold. One by one, I could hear the rocks hitting the ground as its eyes pulled me further into its hypnotic trance, leaving me only with the sense of hearing. But the sense of hearing was enough, as the wind seemed to fill the forest with howling cries. So loud were the cries of the crows that the branches quivered.

In an instant, the entity was gone. Knowing what I know now, it had every advantage over me. It was at this young age that I realized our world was a very strange place.

The unusual thing about these beings is they appear to cast a shadow or so it seems. In truth, their bodies hold two spirits, one always shielding the other. Undetected in the darkness, their spirits are capable of travelling over a vast area. Although the sky travellers seem to be just passing through this land from time to time, our ancestors believed these creatures needed a place to house their spirit while on earth. We don't believe their bodies can exist in our world. If they can, it's not for long.

"With the thick forest and the early morning fog that blankets this area, our hunters wouldn't think one day was any different from the next, until they are face to face with one of them," Isaac warns.

Like Horace, many of the men that went missing in those days were sighted off and on for a while, but they never came home after that time. Rekindling these stories does bring to mind the spoken words of our great-great grandfathers.

"Yotká:teh tsi saka:ratonh tyoht konh enhonnehyá:ra'ne." (Tell these stories often so that they should never be forgotten).

Something Is in the Clouds

"It's not just the mist on the ground we now have to worry about," Silas anxiously speaks up. "Tell the story of your neighbours," he urged his uncle Gilbert.

Silas always found himself shaking inside when hearing these stories, facts he knew he just couldn't ignore. Whether he was ready or not, his inner soul was preparing him. One day his mind would tap into that other existence, not because he wanted to, but because it was all around him. He was already having dreams, forewarning him of the danger of things to come. Odd feelings he couldn't shake when crossing paths with someone he just met. Visions he hadn't quite understood.

Silas sluggishly stretched out his arms and then his legs and silently complained the log was not quite high enough. Slowly, he finds comfort as he leans forward, his lower arms now resting over his knees as he waits for his uncle to begin.

Gilbert smiles, his eyes seem to have a twinkle to them.

His brother Carter laughs as he jokingly tells Gilbert, "Don't even tell that story of how you met your wife."

When the kidding and laughter subsided, Gilbert wiped the sides of mouth with the inside of his shirt and amusingly brushed the crumbs from the length of his top as he begins.

"I was just a young man when I built my house."

He gave a slight nod as he acknowledges his brother's help. There weren't more than four homes on that stretch of dirt road. My nearest neighbour was about a quarter mile away. He would tell of a yellowish-orange glow that had often appeared in the woods behind my house.

A few years had passed without seeing a thing. Then one late August when daylight hadn't quite settled in the evening sky. I began to see a strange blanket of fog crawling along the length of the forest. I sat and watched for a time out of curiosity. It was when a yellowish-orange glow lit up the forest; it wasn't long before it led some of our men into that area.

The men stayed low, their rifles by their side. It was here among the trees that some claimed there was movement along the bark of the trees. Unsure of what they were looking at, the hunters did what any one of us would have done, they dug in and hid under the damp leaves and twigs, and they watched.

They claimed they saw small strange looking figures moving within the bushes, but couldn't be sure, as their skin seemed to blend in with the fog. It soon became clear just what they were looking at when the small figures passed in front of the bark of the trees it caused a fusion together. Their skin was partly visible. These odd shaped figures with large heads seemed to be collecting soil or plant life along the ground.

It was a shift in the fog that next had us running. The fog began to swirl around them. Any dead branches were tossed in the air as if by a powerful wind. When they looked back the yellowish-orange light was gone and so were the odd shaped figures. Gilbert chuckles as he makes light of his story.

"Like the Little People. There are enough people that say they are real, but you will never find them."

"How would you know when these beings are there?" Beth questioned. "In any given day you wouldn't think any of these clouds or mist was unusual."

"*The mist moves in an unnatural way,*" Isaac said as his head slightly turns catching the uncertainty in Beth's face.

"The most recent time was about twenty years ago," Gilbert continued.

It was a clear summer night. Amelia lived a few houses down the road along with her two sons and small daughter. After a late supper, Amelia had no sooner filled the dishpan than her oldest son David asked to visit next door with his friends. To watch for any shooting stars he had said. It was only a five-minute walk between the two backyards and knowing how hot it was the last few days, the cool night air would probably help them sleep. She agreed if he took ro'kénha' (his younger brother). David quickly rushed his younger brother Ned out the door.

"Maybe I'll come and join you when I'm finished," she called out from the kitchen door.

The two brothers quickly ran next door and climbed in the back of an old truck that had sat in their backyard for as long they could remember. Finding an empty space on an old blanket, his friends pointed out the constellations they knew, and if it was wrong no one cared. It wasn't long before they settled back scanning the heavens in silence with their endless imagination.

It was David who noticed the three white fluffy yotsha:ta (clouds) in the night sky, each about five feet long and just as wide. The clouds floated down just inches from the roof of the neighbour's home. The children laughed with excitement as the clouds slowly floated in sequence just above them and always high enough so the children couldn't touch them.

It was when David stepped down from the truck that one of the clouds pulled away from the others.

"I'll be right back." David called out to his brother as he hurried across the backyard.

Amelia could hear David calling out to her as he made his way to the back door. "You have to see this," his voice was almost a loud whisper as he held his face against the screen on the door. David knew something wasn't right he felt it in the pit of his stomach. Whatever David knew about clouds, clouds never float down and position themselves above you.

"I'll be done in a few minutes. Just wait!" Amelia called back.

She smiled as she thought about the excitement in his voice. Her sons seemed to always find the most unusual things, she thought. Like the snakeskin David found lying next to a pile of tree stumps, or the tree toad his brother Ned witnessed camouflaging itself against the tree bark. She smiled to herself as that memory is quickly pulled away.

"óksak (quickly), it can't wait!" David persisted as he held the door open.

She quickly dried her hands on an old tattered towel that was draped over the chair. When Amelia stepped outside, David immediately pointed to the high bushes that lined the footpath.

"satkah yohsereh i:ih tsi nonwe kanonhsaktatye," (Look, it followed me along the side of the house) David said surprised that it had now positioned itself just over the bushes. He tells his mother how the three clouds had floated above them. When asked how long the clouds were sitting overhead David was unaware of the time that had passed.

Amelia not wanting to frighten her son, pointed out it might be vapour from the factories in the nearby town. The wind must have caught the mist in an updraft and carried it here, she suggested. Still she knew what she was looking at was unusual. In her culture, she was also taught that the spirit world does exist and they come through from time to time. And for a moment, she remembers the words of her grandmother, as she stood shaking as a little girl, pleading to understand what she had seen.

"Kénhak (Let it be). Let them pass."

Still Amelia can't shake that unnerving feeling, as she watched the cloud move whenever they moved.

"It's just a cloud. It will just float away. You'll see," she said trying to make light of it.

At that moment, David asked to go back to sit with his friends as that unsettling feeling in his stomach had disappeared. But this time, the cloud didn't move, as it now seemed to be watching Amelia. She found herself wanting to touch this strange cloud, but knowing not to. It was here Amelia now felt uneasy. She found herself trying to block what she was thinking, not wanting it to know her thoughts, as if it had an existence. She pulled away stepping back inside the safety of her home as she could not shake that feeling it could possibly have a power over her. There was something odd about this cloud.

It was through the screen door that Amelia now kept a watchful eye on her sons. Although the cloud never seemed to turn itself around, it began to move in the direction of the children. Amelia quickly called out as calmly as she could, while keeping in mind this cloud had intelligence.

"It's getting late. It's past your bedtime," she called out to the children.

As they returned to their homes, the clouds simply floated away. A number of years passed and they never mentioned the strange clouds again. It wasn't until Amelia had her second encounter, that she connected the unusual clouds.

Amelia woke in the middle of the night with a strange yellow glow in her room. She felt herself in a panic, with a sudden urgency to check on her youngest son Ned. Her first thought was, did he make it back as was promised? He was there fast asleep. Within minutes after returning to her own bed the light slowly faded.

When Ned woke that same morning he told of a strange dream. He dreamt that he was in the field not far from home. A large bush seemed to be centred in front of him a short distance away. Although he never saw any lights the large bush seemed to glow. He stayed low hiding himself against the ground as a thick fog now blocked most of his view. When he looked again several figures appeared out of the fog. Although they were looking in his direction, he felt they were unconcerned.

Strange part that morning; his shoes were sitting just inside the back door, still wet from the early morning dew.

"Ever since I heard that story, I unconsciously take a quick look towards the sky, day or night," Gilbert chuckled. He chuckled again as he makes eye contact with his brother and sister as an old memory comes to mind.

"Remember our father as well as grandfather would scold us if we didn't scan our surroundings before stepping out the door or into the woods. Maybe he meant more than wild animals," Gil laughingly said.

"Stories can come throughout a lifetime from our families and friends, even strangers if you take the time to listen," Isaac said.

It's not uncommon among our people to hear stories from time to time, of unusual lights in the sky, or clouds that seem out of place on a clear day. Or the Little People, they have been sighted off and on for hundreds of years. They are startled as much as we are when we meet in path. Hearing a sudden snap of a twig, and they're gone.

Just like it's not unusual to hear stories of someone walking along on the road in the late hours of the night and having that unnerving feeling you're not alone. Before long you'll begin to hear footsteps that can't be explained. Or stories of friends or family members that aren't the same any more after walking alone after dark.

"There could be many reasons why spirits still linger here," Isaac said. "We must remember other clans have roamed along the river for thousands of years, settling for a length of time and then moving on. It's likely many of the spirits we hear and see have existed here long before we settled in this land."

We have all heard stories of spirits lingering a time after a loved one's death. Some, we believe, stay a year after their death while others believe they return periodically throughout our lifetime. In time their memories fade. They may still be there, but we can't feel their existence any longer. That existence is so close.

"Let them pass. Pay them no heed," Isaac said.

"We don't doubt their stories are real. Too many of our people have heard and seen these strange things," Carter said.

Carter sat up straight and arched his back. "I don't believe things are completely right, not yet," Carter said as he caught Isaac's glance and then Emily's. "There's something else you need to be aware of," Carter said in a concerned voice. "I have sat and spoken with many of our people along the river. It was the day you went missing," Carter said reminding Emily of the last time he had seen her at the Gathering along the river. "Many changes have come about in our territories, from east to west and into the United States," Carter continued.

"Stories of strange unexplainable things, we now understand the reason and reports of the ghostly spirits sighted through our community after talking to Isaac. But there is something else, a large upright creature. Some said this being stood seven or eight feet high, with long hair all over its body. It fears no one."

Isaac shook his head in agreement.

There is a legend that tells of a creature similar to the story of the two brothers. They come into our world from time to time. They say this creature comes to retrieve the evil spirits that have entered into our world through the practise of bad medicine. These evil spirits cling to the most innocent, tormenting the young while they sleep, even babies.

The interesting thing about this creature is - it won't help the person that brought out these entities into our world. Jealousy and greed has marked these people. Some believe this longhaired creature will come back into our world at the time of their death taking their spirit to the underworld. If these longhaired creatures are back, there could be only one reason, to rid us of any evil spirits.

I was fascinated with their stories and eager to hear more, but could see Emily fidgeting around in the corner of my eye.

"The Gathering my brother spoke about is coming to an end in a few days," Emily said. "It's like a different world at this time of the year with so many different clans coming into our territory. You should come along, bring your sons. Maybe we can get some answers to your past."

For a moment, Beth recalls sitting with Isaac as he lay in bed recovering from the dog attack, and finds out her great-grandfather was a Native man, first cousin to a man named Jeremiah Hill, a Turtle Clan from the Mohawk Nation (ancestor to the Jacket family).

In that moment, a smile pulled across her face. Beth was close to finding out how she fit into their strange world.

Emily said no more about the Gathering, but picked up her belongings.

Beth quickly told the others she hoped to see them at the Gathering, and hurried along following Emily through the bushes.

"Did something happen back there. Why did we leave so quickly?" Beth questioned.

Emily laughed lightly, "Why! They can see we are leaving."

Emily's suddenness was going to take some time getting used to. I agreed to go to the Gathering and began to make plans with Emily.

The Gathering

Upon arriving, my sons anxiously danced around me as an array of colourful headdresses passed in front of us.

"Are these people our relatives?" my son whispered.

"Some might very well be," Beth said while looking for Emily in the small crowd that now seemed to be rushing through the gateway. Unknown faces, yet she felt a comfort like she had always belonged here. A satisfying smile spread across her face as she searched her surroundings.

It looked more like an old fort with the unfinished logs standing six feet high. For a long moment, Beth let her mind wander home. She found herself as a child standing along the fence line with her father just behind their home. He was replacing several logs that had long ago rotted away.

Unanswered questions began to fill Beth's mind. It didn't make sense for her father to scold her of the dangers of crossing over the fence line. Or the fact that he moved so close to the Sacred Forest. Why had he returned when he did? What had happened that he couldn't tell us any part of his life? After all, he was a part of this strange world I was just beginning to know.

Startled from my thoughts, Emily was now standing beside me. Her voice was loud with excitement.

"Many families have already gathered along the river," Emily said.

At that moment, Emily reached out taking Beth's arm and began to hurry Beth and her sons through the crowd. Beth could see several young men in a clearing playing a game of ball of sorts. A net attached to a long stick, they tossed the ball with a speed she never saw before. Many stood watching as a small crowd had already formed to cheer them on.

"More than likely the attsihkwá:'eh (lacrosse game) will continue most of the day," Emily said.

"It's also a time to sell or trade the things we worked on so diligently all year, but mostly it's a time for our Elders to come together to learn of any changes in our territory and theirs. Even the flow of water along the creeks will give us warnings with so many changes in the outside world. We already know there are plants we'll never see again. Warnings we always have to be aware of.

Our Elders hold the most respected positions in our communities, as they are our wisdom keepers. They are the ones who teach our traditions and help guide our children through their developing years.

"These teachings should never be forgotten," Emily said with a sombre tone. "I first began coming to these Gatherings when I was just a little girl," Emily said as she looked over a crowd of dancers just below them. "It wasn't as large as it is today."

For a long moment a smile spread across my face as I looked onto the faces of the dancers. And for a long moment, I felt their enthusiasm as the women dancers adjusted their sleeves and straightened the waistline of their traditional dresses, for the drums had begun.

"It is a time for our people from different territories to come together," Emily said. Some travel for miles just to see their relatives at this time of the year. Still, to some people it's a chance to see old friends.

"It's like a celebration."

Emily gave a thin smile as she motions Beth and her sons to follow her along the twisted path leading throughout the trees. Hundreds of people littered the large clearing just below them. An obvious setting for their ceremonies as the river ran the length of it. The trees and small brushes that surround this clearing seem to offer that all that enter will be protected. You could feel the excitement moving through the crowd in minutes as the drums continued to beat. The children quickly found their parents, as the colourful event was to begin.

"It's best we find some shade. It's going to be a long day," Emily warns.

We quickly found a suitable spot, like many others. With the tall trees that littered the embankment, we settled between three huge maples. I was glad we took Emily's advice and brought a couple of blankets. Without another thought my sons had cushioned themselves next to me, their eyes eager to see more.

It was here between the huge maples and the slow movement of the river that I found peacefulness inside of me.

"I told you yóhskats kentho (it was beautiful here)," Emily said.

I watched as a slight breeze caught the length of Emily's pepper grey hair, and for a long moment her eyes closed as a cool breeze fell against her skin. She had found her own serenity. A forgotten time if only for a moment, a memory she had always had etched in her mind, wahon:nise' kenha tsi kahyonhaktatye wa'onkwarohroke ayakwakhon:ni kakhwi:yohs (a youthful time when her people gathered along the banks of the river while preparing food for their families).

"When I was a little girl, it was the most exciting time of the year," Emily said.

Friends and relatives would often travel hundreds of miles to get to the Gathering, and as always old friends would stop by to visit my parents at our home at that time. Several families had children we had never met, and it wasn't uncommon for them to have large families, some up to twelve children, sometimes more. The small children would bunch together sharing the same bed, while corn-husk mats were laid out for others. My parents would not hesitate to give up their bed, and would often sleep on the floor as old winter coats and hides were often laid out.

On this particular summer night, along with khe' ké-nha' (my younger sister), we shared a niwá:'ah tsi yonon-hwétstha' (small bedroom) in the upstairs loft. I remember waking in the middle of the night with the sound of loud knocking on the back door. Startled from our sleep, we were still shaking as we crawled off the bed to hear who was in our home. Slowly, we would tiptoe down that old plank stairwell all the while avoiding any splinters in our bare feet, as the planks were not quite worn down on the edges in those days. We would find ourselves trembling as we strained to listen to the strange occurrences. Ghostly things in our community and theirs, some stories we had heard before, ne nahoténhson (like the things) wàhatiken (people saw) and felt. But this night was different. The late knock on the door brought an old friend named Gerard from the Shotinontowane'hà: kah (Seneca Nation). A man that often spoke the Mohawk language whenever he was in our ter-ritory. And it wasn't uncommon for different tribes to pick up a different language while lodging in other territories.

Mother had moved the large pot of stew to the centre of the wood stove. It wasn't unusual to leave it to slow cook all day. We would help ourselves whenever we were hun-gry. My mother would also make a niyohontéhsha' kah-nekákonh (strawberry drink) at that time of the year and sweeten it with some of the wáhtha' óhshehs (maple syrup) she had wa'onteweyèn:ton tsi nikariwehs kohsera'kè:neh (put away for the winter).

When the meal had ended and the drinking jar sat empty by his bowl, Gerard seemed uncertain in what he wanted to say. Several times he had run his hand along his jawbone. Finally, he began to tell a story of odd sounds at night that couldn't be explained in his house. Faint sounds of small voices and things darting around, but never seen.

Little People

Ni hononkweta:a nihonno:sa (Little People), hearing these words we began to shiver as if the stairwell had suddenly turned cold. My parents sat up straight in their chairs, but never said a word. To some of our people it was never spoken of. Some believe they can change form to hide where they are, even in a simplest thing as a mushroom or unusual plant, while others believe the Little People step away through another existence, gone in a blink of an eye.

The stories have always been there and every once in a while someone will sit next to you, reminding you they never left this land.

For a moment Emily smiled, "I can still hear grandmother's warning to never crush any mushrooms."

"It all began one late spring day," Gerard said as he began to take us back to the day his brother and his family had returned home after years of working throughout the States. His seventeen-year-old son Kale was happy to return, along with his eight-year-old sister. By the time his parents had driven past the unseen margin line to the Seneca's territory an inner peace had settled inside of him, as if the atmosphere had suddenly stabilized. Gerard was pleased to have them stay with his family till they found another place.

That night, Kale could hardly wait till the sun came up. He quickly scribbled on a paper that morning, "Fishing." Packing all he could hold he headed for the creek. It didn't matter how many times he went fishing he always had that same thought, catching the biggest fish. At seventeen, it wasn't unusual for him to fish all day or would it be unusual for him pitch a tent overnight.

As the night crept on, he could have sworn he was hearing the faint sounds of children singing. Tiny voices and it wasn't far from his tent. He knew what sounds the forest could make. He had heard the small dead branches and twigs drop periodically from the trees while walking through the woods. And it wasn't unusual to hear small animals moving throughout the night. Believing it wasn't anything other than the darkness playing tricks with his mind, finally he laid back as the sounds of the forest slowly drifted away.

When morning arrived he found small tracks, although peculiar looking they lead him up over a small hill. Before he realized how far he had walked he was now lost. The land was not how he remembered it. Here he sat and listened for a time, but it wasn't the sounds of the forest that could help, but the damp sandy soil around him. These imprints were made by buckskin, with two defined markings on its heels. It was in the shadows of the forest that he now sees a young man. He couldn't be much older then himself he thought. He quickly calls out to him.

"Can you help me find my way? I seem to be lost."

The young man never said a word. Kale hurried along all the while calling out to the young man. The faster he ran he couldn't catch up. Then just as he stopped to catch his breath he hears a small branch snap. In the bushes, he sees the small child dart away beneath the branches.

"Ka ní:se nontáhse" (Where did you come from)? Kale calls out.

Laughter quickly trailed behind the small child. Seeing the height of the child, it couldn't be more than two years old he thought. Concerned for the child, he questioned the young man's odd behaviour. Why would he leave a child in the woods? Then just as the branches parted, his mouth dropped. It wasn't the face of a child as he thought, but kakónhsa' (a face) of roksténha (an old man). His nose was somewhat long with a small crease running across his nose. His mouth quickly gathered into a pucker, while his small beady eyes grew at the suddenness of being found. As quickly as the small man turned his head, he was gone.

Determined to find this strange little man Kale dropped to his knees as he felt his way through the undergrowth. Again my nephew came face-to-face with this strange little man. The little man wasn't afraid, as he had settled himself against a log. He quickly wiped his hand under his nose as the small crease on top of his nose deepened. Kale couldn't believe what he was seeing. The stories were real. It was amongst Kale's thoughts that the little man waited for just the right moment. In a blink of an eye, the little man was gone.

At that moment Kale remembered a story his mother once told when she was a child. She was playing on the floor one morning, and when she looked up a little man was standing there watching her from the window ledge. The little man's head pulled back. His eyes grew in disbelief. She claimed he was there long enough to see he was an old man. His clothes were an odd green as was his hat. Within seconds he turned and darted away. Strange things began to happen in their home after that time.

"Remembering the story of his mother, my nephew should have run out of the woods," Gerard said.

It was often said that there are two types of Little People. Some are kind, while others are mischievous. They have a dark side to them. Some people believe they can look into your mind knowing everything about you.

"So if you happen to see one, leave them alone," Gerard warned.

Kale did remember the stories, but there were other stories of Little People helping when a person became lost, leaving food and water. It was that thirst to know that the warnings he was taught as a child fell from his thoughts, never to follow these Little People.

Again he is pulled from his thoughts. He hears that same small voice singing just over a high ridge. Slowly he pulls himself over the tangled roots and down the rocky terrain. What he saw was beyond belief, Little People working diligently behind prying eyes. They seemed to be preparing for winter because raonathereó:konh kanà:nonh (their baskets are full), but in a snap of a twig they were gone. Again he was left confused. There were no tracks anywhere, no proof they were even real. But just as his foot sifts through the sand he finds a small clay bowl.

When he arrives home, he tells his parents what he had seen. To his surprise, he is scolded for following them. He is warned to never tell a soul where they are.

"They will never let you sleep."

Still he disregards his parents and tells his friends. They make plans to meet at the campsite the next day.

The next morning, Kale wakes to an empty house. Here he finds a note. "Will be back tomorrow morning."

It's here in the stillness of the house he hears a faint sound of scratching at the front door, then the windows. Things are now being tipped over or out of their place. As the hours pass and the sun is settled in the evening sky, things began to move in the cupboards and closets. He runs frantically through the house, but there is no one there.

Then just as he is about to give up he hears movement in his sister's room. His sister's room is in turmoil as if she had been looking for something. He questions her behaviour and why their parents have left her at home without telling him. It was here he see something in his sister's eyes that wasn't quite right. She began to question him, saying peculiar things that his sister wouldn't know. For a long moment, he watches as a slow disturbing smile spreads across her face. Shaking, he steps from her room with the most unsettling feeling. It's here in his thoughts. He connects his sister's odd behaviour to the little man he believed was running through his uncle's home.

It's in that same moment, he hears a small voice laughing just outside her bedroom window. Without hesitation, he runs out the back door and leaps off the back steps. There he hears the sound of rustling leaves just under the small bushes. For a moment he looks back at his uncle's home. He pulls the fear from his thoughts as he crawls amongst the shadows of the small bushes and undergrowth. Feeling the sharp stones digging into his knees he questions why he is even crawling in the darkness after all he knew where they lived. At that moment a branch snaps back slapping him in the face.

Then the most peculiar thing happens, he finds himself back at the same ridge. Again he pulls himself down the rocky terrain to get a closer look and as he does the extraordinary thing began to happen. Unaware of the time that has passed, it is now daylight. An earlier time in history is now showing before him.

He sees a village of Little People. Their faces hold the dread they are feeling. Dark clouds begin to fill the sky as the deafening kwa yorakahreh tsi yoweronh (thunder roars) a'eren eh niyo:re (in the distance). The lightning sparks a brightness so brilliant it lights up the earth around them. Tsiok nahoten ta:we (Something was coming), more deadly tsi ní:yoht ronónha iken' rontkahthos (than they could imagine). Amidst the thundering, roars Kale could hear loud voices shouting as men and women are coming with heavy footsteps. He can see their hands waving in the air with clubs and pitchforks. He turns to see many of these Little People fall from their injuries.

A small white haired woman was now standing next to Kale. She warns him to quickly hide. He watches the Little Men gathering their families to the hollows between the rocks.

In the next instant Kale wonders out loud, "What's happening to me?"

Kale is now being pulled into the cave, his size no bigger than the Small Men beside him. Fear races through his mind as screams of terror echo throughout the cave.

Loud voices begin to fill the cave as Kale is told of their suffering in those days.

"The people with heavy footsteps only see us as horrid to look at. They believe we will lead their children away. When we came out of the cave wa' teyakwatteni (we changed). We no longer run and hide, but have the ability to hide within our surroundings. What you see is only what we want you to see."

It was in that time after some of our men became so spiteful. They lost the ability of kindness and forgiveness. It is that kindness and the ability to forgive what holds our village together. Kale is warned of the tricks that will continue to be played on him and any others like him.

"We ask you to never tell a soul where we are," the white haired woman said.

When Kale looks back, he is lying under the bushes in his uncle's backyard. It's here amongst his cloudy thoughts he hears his parents calling out to him. When he turns, he sees his sister standing there.

'Whether it was a dream or not, Kale took it as a warning," Gerard said.

At that moment, Beth turned as she could feel her son move even closer.

"They can't be real!" Beth questioned.

An unsettling smile crossed Emily's face. You can search for miles, but you will never find one Little Person.

When I was a young girl, I didn't believe they were real until one day while going fishing with my brother. His steps were long as I tried to catch up. In an instant, ne nihra:a ronkwe (a Little Man) ran across the path two steps behind my brother. My brother never saw a thing, but could hear a rustling sound as the bulrushes parted just beside him.

"They continue to live among our people to this day," Emily added. "That story of Kale has always stayed with me. Ever since that time, I go to the yearly Gathering and every once in a while if I'm lucky, someone will share one of his or her stories of nihonna:sa onkwehó:konh (Little People)," Emily said.

The crowd had now grown in size by this time as Emily finished her story. I had noticed several different headdresses and was about to ask Emily the reason for this. Then Emily began to point out the different clans from other Native communities that arrived for the Gathering.

Some came from as far away as British Columbia and the United States. For many it was their first time taking a train. There would be many stops, as Elders from other territories will be boarding along the way. Their plan was to stay for the week or two if at all possible. It was a tiring time for our Elders. Wakenya'tathén (I have been thirsty) and tahnon waktonhkaryake (I was hungry) several of the Elders said as the step down from the train. Many didn't foresee the length of their journey.

"They had joked, they will need a bigger bag of food for their return," Emily said with a chuckle. "Our Native visitors had set up camp earlier in the week, while others made plans months ahead of time to stay with friends they had made from previous visits to our territory," Emily went on to say.

It is a mile walking distance from my home. And it wasn't long before I could hear the drums in the distance beating a familiar sound. I found myself hurrying along as their wailing voices echoed throughout the forest. The ceremonial fire had begun. It is a chance for our people to sell or trade their beadwork or their beautiful ribbon shirts and leggings, traditional dress for our Mohawk people. Many would work all year on their buckskin jackets and vests in hope of a good turnout. Still others came with their soapstone carvings, held true with every curve.

It's a time to visit old friends and to meet other clans from other territories. A time for our leaders to come together, to keep in touch with the ever-changing world that surrounded our territories. It was in these times that I realized we share a bond with each other, whether it's in the food we prepare or in our spiritual belief.

"I have seen many changes over the years, many good changes," Emily went on to say. "The kenea ken (non-Native people) you see have arrived from different communities to marvel at the dancers and the colourful, feathered kahstòserako:wa' (headdresses). They are all unique to their own tribe," Emily said with a smile as she leaned back once again against the trunk of the tree.

When the long day had ended and twilight had left a blush of bluish grey tint against the sky, a noticeable hush fell over the scene that stood in front of me. I watched the parents gather up their weary children as they headed back to their small towns. This land was no longer filled with mistrust or uncertainty. The savagery once told by their grandparents was no longer in their minds. When I turned back again, I saw their small heads glance back seizing their own memory of this day. A warm smile spread across their parents' faces as they load their children onto small benches that lined the back of their trucks.

Many of our people who were in walking distance or had the means for a ride home stayed behind carrying raona'there'ó:konh (their baskets) and raonahsire'ó:konh (their blankets) to settle closer to the river. Although it was never said or made known, it was understood. It was a chance to hear the news from the other dancers and their families that had travelled from so far away. Some of the younger men scattered around finding fallen branches from the last winter storm to start a fire.

It wasn't long before some of the elderly women and men stepped from the wooded lot where they sat most of the afternoon, keeping out of the hot sun. Slowly they made contact, but only with their eyes as they searched for familiar faces. Out of respect, several of the young pulled their cornhusk mats and blankets back leaving a space so their elderly grandparents would be closer to the fire as the night grew on. Our elderly people haven't got used to the crowds that these events bring, but they know it was a chance for our people to trade or sell their crafts.

"And it's a time to see their old friends and relatives," Emily added.

The children quickly huddled inside the blankets with their parents and grandparents, as the evening air pulled us all a little closer. A woman began passing around a basket of teyona'taratsikhe:tareh (sweet bread), which she had tucked away earlier in the day. As well, someone brought some cooked venison. "wákewa:rarihte ne ohskennon:ton" (I cooked the deer meat), a man said with a smile. Large pieces were cut and handed out among the growing crowd that was forming within the light of the fire. Friends and families laughed and joked with each other as they reached out to break off a piece of kanatarakeri:ta (fry bread) that was being passed around. They laid out their handkerchiefs across their laps, while others hurriedly spread out much larger cloths on the ground.

I watched and listened as one family stood out above the rest. The woman's voice was very low if she spoke at all, but the children understood as they eagerly reached over to straighten the frayed ends of the blanket. Their mother seemed to smile as the frayed ends touch the back of her hand. That old rolled up blanket seemed to waken some old memories, memories she had too long kept buried inside.

For a long moment more, her eyes were held against her blanket. Isn't it strange when you find a memory that can touch your soul, waken the love you once felt so long ago.

I continued to watch the delight on their small faces. Their hopes put a stir in the air as they watched the basket of sweet bread still being passed around. Some of the children stood up keeping a watchful eye. At last their small outstretched hands clutched together.

A white haired woman, named Hazel, slowly made her way down the path that entwined throughout the tall maples. She was well known for her (lyed corn), and kanenhstohare (hot corn soup) was good at any time of the year. She smiled as she looked over the crowd. Many had anticipated and brought a canning jar or at least yenontararáhkwa' (a soup bowl). Slowly she laid out her hand-stitched quilt. Her children quickly found their favourite pattern as it was arranged just so.

A number of families turned her way in hopes that she had brought along some of her delicious kanátaronkhón:we (corn bread). They watched as she reached into an old flour sack she had been carrying. The small crowd stirred ever so slightly, and almost as gentle as a whisper their heads nod once with approval.

It was no shame of being hungry or would there be any shame of not having anything to share with the others. When their stomachs were full, the small children once again nestled next to their mothers and grandparents. Their eyes drearily finding sleep as they watched the flame leap into the night sky.

Emily was the one that spoke first, introducing my sleepy children as well as myself. Their smiles were felt as I looked over the crowd. Still many never looked up, but I had seen them glancing periodically in my direction. The low laughter had by now subsided as many of the grandparents glanced in the direction of their teens.

"The stories will only be told once," Beth heard one say.

It was something about their Elders that Beth had noticed before. The teenagers had a great respect for the old in this community. She hoped it would never change. Their voices now fell silent amidst the dim light of the fire as Emily began.

"Most of us have lived our whole lives in this community. Many have sat and listened in the late hours of the night as our grandparents retell the stories that have been passed down through their grandparents. Unbelievable things, dark shadows that seem to trail along the ground, but have no eyes. Or the dark shadows that can stretch themselves along the wall only to disappear through the ceiling. Some have seen thin dark figures with human shapes, their features you will never see. They hide in the corner of your eyes. Some you will see leaning outward peeking at you from the edge of a wall. While others are standing tall watching you, when you turn to get a closer look they're never there. Still you'd swear you saw something crouching in the low bushes. Shadow people, you will never see their true form."

"Footsteps or the sound of faint whispers you thought you heard when entering a room. For some it's a feeling as if someone is near you or the feeling of a hand as it touches your shoulder. But as always you will never see them. Amazing stories from our past and the present. It's at this time of the year we like to share some of our stories from our territory and yours."

Something Isn't Right
With the Animals

We could hear one of the men not far away. His voice was somewhat loud, as he takes the lead to be first.

My name is Clay. There was an unusual dog sighted around my place. The other dogs would become aggressive when it was near, but none would attack, not even when the dog ate their food. The men in our area tried chasing it away with sticks, but it wouldn't move. It had the strangest brown eyes, kwa nene okara ne ronkwe (like the eyes of a man). The men all felt there was an evil presence about this animal.

Then the most peculiar thing began to happen. Things they weren't especially proud of over the years began to show up in their minds, taking away the confidence they felt about themselves. The men would cower away leaving the strange animal. Others complained their minds began playing tricks on them when the dog was near. Most said they didn't know what they were looking at. They just couldn't agree on what kind of animal it was.

The animal's appearance was odd. Its nose and jaw-bones were similar to a possum. The top of its head was twisted out of shape. And what was more frightening, it walked on the back of its paws while its long toes pulled together in a cluster. Its thin body and patches of long, tangled grey hair suggested it was just a sick érhar (dog), but believe me it's not what it appeared to be.

A young girl was returning home from a friend's house in that same week and may have seen that same animal. Though the sun was setting in the evening sky she wasn't afraid, after all she had walked from her friend's house many times. And it wasn't long before the moon kindly lit up the road in front of her. She smiled to herself, as her thoughts were elsewhere; certainly not what was just ahead of her. She hadn't walked much further when she heard something moving in the ditch beside her. It was in that same moment a strange disfigured animal steps out from the ditch, and for a moment longer she questions what she is looking at amongst the shadows of the bushes. This kário yoti:wenh (thin animal) was now moving in her direction. Its presence and irregular movement horrified her. It was when its eyes turned red and hearing that low growl that sent her running. Her high pitch screams only faded into the darkness, as she realized no one lived in this area.

But no matter how fast she ran she could feel it on the back of her heels. When she reached her laneway an unsettling smile fell across her face, that strange looking animal was nowhere in sight. Caution now pulled at her from every direction, as she strains to listening for any movement in the high weeds beside her. Slowly she exhales believing she is safe now. Still her unusual long laneway uttered something else in her mind iktakhenóntye' (keep running). A slight cry escaped from her mouth as she frantically raced to the front door.

Yet in that same instant she knows her mother always locked the doors at night, and as she reaches for the door handle she distinctly hears movement at the corner of the house. She desperately pounded her fist against the door as she screamed for ako'nihsténha' (her mother) to let her in. Suddenly a chill runs up her back and in that same instant she could feel her head slowly turns to the edge of the house. What she saw was beyond belief. That same animal, although much taller than she would of thought was now standing upright at the edge of the house. Whatever it was that followed her home that night, her parents could see she was physically shaken?

Strange appearances were happening in our territory at that time, it was like a gateway had opened. In that same week, a group of children were walking home from their teachings when they noticed a black figure of an animal sitting high in a tree. The tree was thinning at the top making the animal's shape more visible, but still they couldn't agree on what it was. The face was almost like a monkey as one girl described it. Light brown hair traced its pale face. It's bulkiness and brushy tail coiled around the lower branch didn't seem to support what another girl had seen only a minute before.

Atí:ronh (A raccoon), one of the others said. But again they pointed out, where were the stripes on its tail. Then the oddest thing happened as it darted away, aonha l:ken (it was nothing other than) a niwà: a kahontsi onkwetá:kon (a small black squirrel).

Ellen

The strangest story I remember was told by Akhsótha' (my grandmother) when I was just a young girl, a woman said as she partly raised her hand while introducing herself as Ellen. I'm Bear Clan from the Oneida Nation she said as she looked into the crowd. She also could speak some Mohawk and gave a slight grin.

Three girls were walking home one late night. Not one star shone in the overcast sky. At times they question their behaviour, why had they been so foolish staying out so long. They hurried along knowing they could be possibly drenched before they arrived home as lightning now lit up the tops of the trees in the distance.

It wasn't long after, that one of the girls began to sense an eerie feeling after they pass an old house that stood not more than ten feet from the road. Its sunken roof only added to the creepy feeling they were now sensing. It was when one of the girls swore she saw three small lights bouncing along the roof. For a moment they whispered to each other while their eyes searched the darkness. It was here one of the girls remembered that old house shouldn't be there, it burned long ago. They ran, faster than they could remember, laughing at their silliness when they stopped to catch their breath. They reached out taking each other's hand as they question if they should take a short cut home. It was here in the darkness they began to hear a familiar sound. A hay wagon pulled by a horse, one said, while another believed it was the sound of a small cart, they question if they should hide in the bushes till it passed. Without another thought a black horse pulling an old cart stopped beside them. They nervously laughed when they question who had been steering the horse. For a moment more they almost laughed again as their innocence hindered what they should be looking for. Out in the darkness they heard the cart shift and it was only then that they could see the outline of a man sitting high in his seat. Frightened of what was unfolding in front of them the two younger girls stepped back, while the oldest girl, when asked climbed up onto the seat next to the stranger.

The strange part of this story is when the pouch she was carrying slipped to the floor of the cart, it was in that speck of time she could have sworn he had hoofs for feet. The next morning, she woke up in a cornfield not remembering how she even got there.

Nenéh kontiksten'okón-ha' (The old women) in our kaná:ta' (village) would often tell the young girls not to walk along the road at night. Sometime the young girls would hear the sound of a woman walking with high heel shoes just behind them. When they would run that sound would quicken just behind them as if the woman was now running. The old women in the village believe the woman in high heels was forewarning of danger if they continue to walk after dark.

It's in these times stories will circle our territory. People seeing shadows in their homes or ghostlike figures, dark mist that can't be explained floating in our homes or hearing three knocks on the door or along the wall where we slept. It wasn't as if these stories were connected. Many times our people kept what they had seen to themself. Not because they feared what their family would think about them, or did they ever question something wasn't right in their head. It wasn't a common thing that happens every day, but every once in a while the spirit world will open, just a little, Ellen said as her eyes make contact with some of her friends.

There Is Something in the Dark

"My name is Gary. I'm Snipe Clan from kayonkwe'hà:kah (the Cayuga Nation)," he said proudly, as Gary had lived most of his life among the Mohawk people.

One night when I was in my late teens, I had stepped outside to go to a nearby shed. On my return I could feel something moving behind me, but I couldn't see a thing in the darkness. Then just as I came to the light of the house, I came face to face with a large kahòn:tsih erhar (black dog) with the strangest red eyes. Its fierce growl was so piercing I couldn't move. I could see it wasn't going to let me pass.

It was at this time my father called out from the back door, "Stay where you are and whatever you do, don't take your eyes off the dog."

I stood for hours outside as my parents stood watch from the inside of our home. My parents knew then they were not just looking at an ordinary dog. They couldn't interfere. When the morning came, the strange dog turned away and began walking down the road. My parents now stood watch from edge of the lane, as it now looked to be cowering away. What was more unbelievable, we never took our eyes off that dog. A short distance away the dog turned back looking right at us.

Slowly his body began to curve. We couldn't believe what we were looking at. It wasn't érhar nek tsi roksténha (a dog, but an old man). Slowly he pulled himself up from the road. His body now crooked with age.

The Old Ones would tell stories of such men or women taking the form of animals to do their bidding. They want something from that family or to do them harm. Most often it would be directed at one of the children in their home. If it fails it will be reversed, leaving the person crippled or gravely ill. It was after that time, my father remembered an older man with greying hair had come to the door a few months before. He asked about land we were living on, believing it was left to him as a child. After several attempts and with no proof he had left in a rage.

"To this day, I believe I had come face to face with a witch of sort," Gary said.

"It was often believed among my parents and grandparents if you see something odd or out of place in your path don't dismiss it, it could take another form."

Emily again looks over the small crowd as she steps forward. "It brings to mind the story that was told by my grandmother. It was customary to honour the young girl in the family with atatá:wih (gift) when she became of age. Her gratitude was held in her never-ending smile that day. Her long awaited, hand stitched atya:tawi (dress) and athsinò:ronh (leggings) were felt even more in her mother and grandmother's hearts as they watched the young girl practise her jingle dance throughout the rooms. But that time would be short-lived as she followed the path through the thickest part of the woods, a path she felt a comfort in.

Halfway there to her friend's house she began to feel uneasy, something was nearby. In the bushes for just a moment, she could see these dark eyes staring back at her, but it didn't move. A large dog she thought and quickly moved along as she recalled grandmother's stories of tsyonathonwí:senh (young women) that have gone missing in some of our territories, an occurrence that has caused unbearable pain to our people for hundreds of years.

"There is always that repeated question. How can we stop this kind of evil?" grandmother would say.

Did the young girl catch something in her predators' eyes that day that didn't feel right or was she fooled by their kindness before being led away? Keep a clear head, always check your surroundings when you step out the door. Never walk alone.

Sometimes it's not what you see in front of you, but where they could be hiding. And remember, it's not the animal that can take on a different form. Sometimes it's a man or a woman in plain sight with animal instincts, their skin holds the most feared predator. If you watch closely you will catch it in their eyes, or hear it in their meaning. They'll come in a different form when no one is around. If you hear their breathing change, it's already too late.

"You couldn't imagine what form that person could become."

To this day, hunters have often returned home telling a strange story of hearing a faint sound of something jingling in the brushes.

Sounds on the Roof

Several logs were tossed into the fire as an elderly woman now stood in front of the crowd.

"My name is Nora."

She nervously clutched her dark red and yellow corn beads that hung around her neck as she began saying that she knew of a similar story. "Not about animals, but odd shaped figures that walk in the night, and terrifying sounds that couldn't be described as real. I was just a little girl when kátken akhsótha' (my grandmother) coaxed us to come and sit with her next to the ó:yenteh yononhsa'tariha'táhkwa' (wood stove)."

The elderly woman immediately held her hands out catching the o'tarihénhsera' né yoyentáthenh (warmth of the dry firewood) as her mind took her back nearly a lifetime ago. And for a long moment the woman could almost make out their faces as her young siblings bunched together on that old hand stitched blanket. For only a glimpse would be allowed.

"Akhsótha' (My grandmother) had taken some of grandfather's wool socks and placed them over the double socks we were already wearing. The winter nights were cold in our draughty old house. Rakhsótha (My grandfather) had stuffed the cracks around the windows and doors with rolled up papers and rags. We had bundled up the best we could, but the cold air would always find its way back in as we shivered under blankets and coats. The house was old and the repairs were getting too numerous for our aging grandfather."

"Our mother worked in a nearby town scrubbing floors and hoped that we would one day build a new home, and grandmother and grandfather would live with us. As you know, it isn't unusual in our Native communities for families to live together throughout their whole life along with their children and grandchildren. Grandmother would say we would know when it was time to build our own home."

The elderly woman paused from her story and chuckled a little when she remembered how crowded their grandparents' home was when they were growing up. "yahónhka' teyenhre teyonhtentyes" (no one wanted to leave). She chuckled again while an uneven laughter spread throughout the small crowd.

"It was when the house was silent that night," the elderly woman continued. "The little ones were fast asleep on their cornhusk mats and blankets, a short distance from our wood stove. We all agreed the large piece of deer hide that was draped over them had kept the little ones the warmest that winter. It was at that time my older sister complained of hearing noises in the night. When she listened closer she could have sworn it was tsi ahsk-wake i:reh ne ron:kwe (a man walking on the roof) akta tsi ken'ta:roteh'(near the chimney) she had said, although his stride was longer than most. My grandmother pushed that thought away, she didn't want to hear any more.

"It might be ne atí:-ronh (raccoons)," she finally said. "You know they're always rummaging around out there."

"It sounded much heavier than a raccoon would be," my older sister said. Her voice implied she wanted an answer.

And there was something else that didn't make sense, his dialect. It was as if she was hearing bits and pieces of words or what she could understand.

My grandmother again seemed uneasy. "My father, your great grandfather would tell stories of seeing odd figures walking in the night. Their voices could only be described as coming from wahonnise'kénha' (a long time ago). These ancient voices were fluent as they describe a time when their spirits were detached from their bodies.

This could only happen if they are killed in battle and left on the ground without proper burial," grandmother said.

Our people found what was left of our warriors. Their bones had been picked clean from birds in that area. Their clothes and the remnants of things they would have carried that day, still beneath them. Still there were other warriors, their bones were found scattered about from the wild dogs. Our people gathered all they could find and carefully wrapped them in blankets. They walked that long journey home carrying their bones to our resting place. A great ceremony was held in their honour. The ancient warriors will forever lie next to the Old Ones.

It was in the months after our ancestors began to hear odd stories. Some of our people claimed to have seen a strange bluish haze that seemed to hang over the burial mound.

Great grandfather would often tell a story of walking home in the middle of the night and seeing strange figures moving within the trees. Upright shapes, their legs are long and spindly. Although great grandfather never saw them up close, to him they looked to be kahstyen'tó:tonh (skeletons). He had guessed thirty or forty, maybe more, their steps awkwardly long and unsteady as they continued from graveyard to graveyard.

Some believed these sightings have been occurring over two hundred years. Still there are others, they believed the bones that were found may have been much older.

A sigh escaped from some of the older men and women as they shook their heads in agreement. Wa'honne-hya:rane kawenna ka'yen (They remembered the old stories).

"It's not something you would ever forget, hearing their teeth snapping together while their hollow bones rattled with every step they took. It runs a chill up your back," an elderly woman said.

I could see Nora was oddly shaken as she sat back down. And I couldn't help but think there was another part of this story that Nora had buried away in her mind long ago.

For a long moment some of those same Elders spoke quietly amongst themselves; they finally raised their heads agreeing there might have been fifty skeletons that were carried home in those days.

"After their bones were laid to rest some of our people began seeing strange thin figures moving long the trail we called Sour Springs. An elderly man spoke up. Our ancestors at that time believed there would be only one reason why spirits had not travelled to the spirit world. Their spirit had leaped to a living body at the time of their death. As time passed they couldn't reconnect.

I do remember another story told by my great uncle. It also happened wahonnise'kénha (a long time ago) a young man said while he adjusted the red handkerchief that was tied around his head. It began one winter night as three men were returning home.

When the smaller man suddenly whispered sotahon-satat "(listen)! Did you hear that sound?"

"Onkwathón:tene eh nahò:ten' wa:waks (I heard something rattle)," another man said.

"Wakathonté:onh (I have heard), it sounds like bones rattling together," the tall man said.

Crouching along the low bushes they found themself near an old burial ground not more than thirty feet away. But something didn't feel right; again they could hear movement, their eyes now straining to see what was in the burial ground. What they saw was beyond belief. Skeletons! This frightening sight had their hearts racing as they watched several skeletons pull themselves up from their graves. It was at that moment the skeletons turned as if they knew someone was there.

The skeletons began leaping back and forth across the path. It was here the men began to see that strange haze that seemed to blanket their bodies, for a moment they stared into the fog like matter and as they did they began to see hollow faces of men and women. These captured souls crying out pleading to be released. Without warning, these skeletons turned and leaped in front of the men. Only one man returned home that night."

"These skeletons will forever walk the path to the river in search for their true spirit," the young man said.

An Eyewitness to the Skeletons

"My name is Tony," the partially grey haired man said. "I don't remember my given name," he began, referring to his Indigenous name. "It was taken from me long ago, as it was with my brothers and sisters. To blend us into society the government had said." Tony gave a slight snicker as he continued. "The farmer my father worked for gave me the nickname Tony Bill, as there was another person with the same name working on the farm. You couldn't work without my new name, or a number," Tony said with a half grin, referring to the social insurance number. "As the years passed, I found work in the New York States where I settled for a number of years before returning home."

It was here I watched as a young man carried a stump through the crowd and sat it next to Tony Bill who gently shook his head as a thank you. The man was somewhat older than I had believed, as the young man now helped him up to his seat.

"I have five sons," Tony said proudly as he grasps the young man's hand. "They are all good sons. I come from a long line of Jacket Hills, from the Turtle Clan," the partially grey haired man said as he continued to massage his left knee. Beth smiled as she looked over the crowd and in that moment she could almost feel the warmth of their kindness as it shone in their faces. Tony Bill had touched many of their lives.

At that moment Beth tries to connect how she is related.

He did say he was a Jacket Hill?"

Emily shook her head in agreement. Beth smiled a thin smile as she realized she had found one of her father's families. Although Beth was related to the Turtle Clan, it would be some time later that Beth would learn the clans are passed down from mother to child.

"Whatever these beings were, for me the stories stopped more than forty-five years ago," Tony continued.

When I was a younger man, I witnessed something very strange on my way home through the woods one night. The moon was full on tsi niwahsontehs kwa yotho:re tsi kohserake:ne (that cold winter night), however a sudden dark cloud had cast a shadow over the night sky, somewhat hampering of my vision. I began to see odd shapes in a clearing. They seemed to have a strange aura around them and they didn't seem to look human, I could see that. At first wa'ketsha:nike (I was afraid). I fell to the ground concealing myself beneath some pine branches as my mind raced to understand what I was looking at, the dead had risen. They had arms and legs, but something wasn't quite right. It was when I began to crouch along the ground to get a closer look that I began to see what I was looking at. They were kahstyen'tó:-tonh (skeletons).

It was at that moment these beings stopped, and almost immediately they turned my way. They could see, but their eyes were not like ours. That strange aura that seemed to cloak their appearance also seemed to create a luminous veil where their eyes should have been. You couldn't imagine the fear I felt when I heard three loud piercing cries thrust a sound so loud the tops of the trees seemed to shudder. Whether that sound was directed at me or not, these beings suddenly became still. Their eyes no longer held that luminous glow as if waiting for the next command.

Without another thought, I pulled myself back beneath the ohnehta'kowa (green pine trees). And as I did, I could hear their teeth begin to snap, their hollow bones clashing together. Several skeletons awkwardly stepped into the woods, their long legs clumsily moving over the dead branches toward me. Again I heard three loud blood curdling screams thrust a sound so loud, for that moment I could almost hear the vibration coming from their vocal cords. How was this even possible? My heart was racing as I fought to stay in control. My fear was so great I believed I would be taken at any moment. It was here amongst my racing thoughts I began to hear the top crust of ice covered snow crackle beneath their uneven footsteps as they now continued to step along the path.

At that instant, I couldn't help but think that piercing cry had ordered them back onto the path. Whatever they were, they continued in the direction of the river.

As far as I know they come up from the ground, always within our burial grounds, and always tsi niwenhnì:tehs (during the month) of enníhska' (February). I never walked that way again," Tony said as he raised his head making eye contact with some of the Elders.

A slight bow of their heads, endorsing that he spoke the truth.

"It wasn't until the day I went to visit his friend Charlie that I learned what I had seen. Charlie's mother had taken him aside one night when he was just a young boy along with his younger brother and his sister Grace. She began to tell of a strange time, a story that to some was unbelievable. She warned that what she was about to tell them, was never to be spoken of again."

"Kahstyen'tó:tonh tsi (Skeletons that) were í:-we' kànyote (walking upright)," his mother had whispered.

"Her fear was so great she believed they would return one night to take one of her family. As a young boy, Charlie didn't know what to think. He believed it was just another story, passed down through the years. Still the family was content knowing they would be visiting family they hadn't seen for some time."

The family set out early in the morning and planned to return home the next day. It wasn't unusual for families to walk for miles in those days. They would travel on foot crossing the frozen creek. Here they would find a trail that would lead the length of the river. And it wasn't long after, before their smiles spread across their face. O-non-ta: keh (On the top of the hill) sat their uncle's cabin.

Staying a little longer than expected, but with full stomachs and good spirits they were on their way back home. It didn't seem that they walked more than a couple of miles when darkness began to fall around them. The night air grew colder than any night Charlie could remember.

With the frigid air, the forest seemed unnervingly quiet. They were left only with the sound of small branches snapping periodically, that and the brittle snow crunching and cracking beneath their áhta' (boots) with each step they took.

Charlie's words continued to unfold in Tony's mind as he takes us back to that cold winter night. "It was when we stopped to make a fire that shonkwa niha (our father) seemed uneasy." We heard the most unearthly sound as three loud piercing cries echoed throughout the vastness of trees.

With the low light of the moon, we strained to see what was ahead of us. Something was wathahines (walking on the path). In a loud whisper our father warned us to stay quiet. "More are coming okwiraktátye (along the bushes)," he whispered. Within minutes you could see a strange bluish haze coming onto the path. An alarming feeling shook the very existence of our soul, while those same loud piercing cries continued to fill our minds. Whatever our father thought it was - our father was terrified. He ordered us back into the woods while he scrambled to put out the fire we now had burning.

"They will be attracted to the light of the fire," our father stammered. "Whatever you hear or see, tesato:tat (stay quiet). They will take atónnhets (a soul)," our father warned.

Charlie could hear his father's voice trembling, his hands awkwardly moving as if he didn't know what to do next. Ro'niha (His father) knew there was a chance he couldn't save his family or have time to warn his brother. Our parents immediately began to bury us under dead branches and ice covered leaves and snow until it resembled a mound. We were never so scared in our lives as we anticipated the worst.

Through the ice and snow Charlie watched as the horde of skeletons walked in their direction. Their movement questioned what Charlie knew to be true. Kahstyen'tó:tonh yah nonwén:tonh (Skeletons never) return to tónn hets (life). It was here we heard a spine-chilling sound as their teeth began to snap and clatter, while their hollow bones continually rattled with every step they took. His mother immediately held her hands over the mouth of his little sister and younger brother silencing their quivering cries. It was something about the skeletons or "ehskin" as my father called them. Had they the power to sense the living? Or was it the shallow breathing escaping through our fingers that they could hear as they stood next to our snow-covered mound.

It was in that same moment the eerie clatter began voicing broken words from an ancient time, fragments of what we could understand.

Through their ancient voice the ehskin (skeleton) began to speak of a time of a great war, e:soh ne rotihsken-hrakéhteh wa'hatiya'tayén:ta'ne' wa'hatikahre:wahte (many of our warriors fell from their injuries). Onkwatonnhets onwataweyate (Our souls leaped) tsi rotiya:takon (into our enemies) rononkwetaksens tsi tkarha:konh wahonatahse-hte (that was hiding in the bushes). When we turned back a lifetime had since passed, we couldn't reconnect.

"Through our ancestors we know they will continually rise and follow in the direction of the river, that flow of water is the substance of life. Its power gives off an energy that will forever flow through their memories," Charlie said.

Many of our people find that same comfort with the serenity of the forest as it cradles our mind when you are troubled.

The lighted campfire, or the light coming from within your home, they will always be connected to the light in search of their spirits. So if you hear them coming, put out any light and if in doubt when you hear the door rattle, don't open the door, Charlie had warned.

Grace couldn't get passed that frightful night. When Grace was old enough, she moved away vowing she would never returned to our territory.

The next day, rake'níha' (my father) learned his brother and raohwá:tsireh (his family) were safe. It was only by chance his brother had stepped outside to royen-takarenyes (draw firewood) from the woodpile. It was here in the frigid air he had the oddest feeling, as the forest grew strangely quiet. The slight breeze he thought he had felt now fell from his thoughts.

Something was coming along the oháhaktatye (pathway) ro'kenha' (his younger brother) had taken only hours ago. He too could hear the lumbering footsteps, and for a long moment he stared along the frozen path. With the low light of the moon he could almost make out the figures. For a moment more, he smiled believing it was his brother and family returning. The uneven walk uttered something in his mind that couldn't be right.

Ehskin!

It was here in the shadows of the trees the older brother hid and watched as the figures grew in numbers. Quietly as he could, he lowered his armful of wood back onto the ground while that alarming feeling bordered his sanity. At that moment, his stomach began to churn, after all it was the month of February. Again he questioned his thoughts telling himself the stories had long past with the death of their grandfather. It was here he felt a cold chill run up his back as these gangly figures continue to fill the pathway. Their bones rattling, their teeth snapping as their jawbones shook with every step. Finding his escape through the back door, he ordered his family to blow out any candles and coal oil lamps. They stayed low barely breathing at times as the family huddled together along the floor. The sound of their snapping teeth and rattling bones wailed a fear deep inside all of them as the horde continued to circle their home. The strange thing, when they woke the next morning there was no footprint as Charlie's brother would have thought. Just an odd disruption in the frozen ground, they believed the ehskin (skeletons) had made while circling the cabin.

The men that dared to follow the path to the river described what they seen that same night. It was almost as if the ehskins were going to war as war clubs and bows were held high. It was in that time the men could have sworn they saw a campfire burning as the ehskins seemed to be dancing in celebration. One by one the ehskins stepped back onto the path, and within seconds that bluish ghost-like matter consumed them.

They say the men who bravely watched from behind the bushes said they could hear their haunting screams long after these strange figures had faded into the night.

When the daylight came, our Elders gathered at the burial grounds. They found only the most ancient sites were disturbed.

The old stories say the ehskins will rise from their grave and travel for miles through our territory, stopping at each burial ground in search of their fellow warriors. The old stories tell us it's a terrifying sight to see their skulls emerge up from the ground their teeth snapping with every turn. These gangly skeletons will forever rise and follow the path to the river in search of their spirit.

We don't know why they walk in the month of February, or how many years before they walk again. Some believe there is only a handful left still trying to connect with their spirit. Still, there are hunters claiming to this day to have heard piercing screams in the night while carrying their o'wahrà:seh (fresh meat) home through the woods, strange almost stick-like figures walking in the woods not more than twenty feet away. It was in those times, the Elders agreed, a ceremony would be held at each burial ground. Our Elders had journeyed from graveyard to graveyard with the intent to walk the ehskins step by step through the spirit world in search for their spirits.

As the years passed, our Elders believed they were finally at rest. But something wasn't right; our people began hearing piercing cries in the thickest part of the forest. Whatever happened we believed some of these ancient souls couldn't connect; they were back. The flow of the river is the only existence they feel while on earth. We believe these skeletons will forever walk in search of their spirit. So remember to keep your fires low. Their piercing cries are described as taking a deep breath while the air thrust from their throat into a blood-curling scream.

"Our Elders always have ways of pulling us into their stories. Before long our imaginations will be running wild," Emily whispered to Beth.

So many of our lessons and cautions were told through stories. Sometimes it is hard to believe these kinds of stories are real. Like I said before, there is a reason why we don't walk over the burial ground.

"There aren't stories like that anymore, right grandmother?" a young girl spoke up while pulling the blanket a little farther over her pant legs.

Many of the old stories passed down from my grandparents have since passed wahonnese konha (a long time ago). Although I do remember a story told more recent. They say there is an old woman who lives deep into the woods. A seer I was told and about a man named Ross that came to seek her advice.

The Seer

They say this konwatya'tonhkwát-kens (fortune teller) could feel an odd feeling whenever she stepped back onto the boundary of our territory. A past existence we thought, but she never would say.

Ross had attended a service held for his beloved uncle. After months of having trouble sleeping he decided he would visit a seer. He didn't know much about the old woman only that she lived alone karhakón (out in the woods) far from the others, so she couldn't hear their thoughts, she had said.

Ross set out walking along a well-travelled path. Although he hadn't walked more than a mile, he grew tired as branches and thorn bushes were making it almost impossible to continue. It was when the path divided he wondered if he should just go back home. When he turned back he finds an old wooden box; there he sat for a while. It wasn't long after before a dark haired woman walked on that same path.

"Do you know what path leads to see the seer's home?" Ross asked.

She oddly began to shield her eyes as if the sun was shining brightly, although Ross could see her shadow stood in front of her.

"i:non nonka:ti ensathonte tewahonrate ne kar-hakónha tsi ni kayato:ton" (You will hear hawk calls out in the distance, follow in its direction), the dark haired woman said. She never said another word, but continued on her way.

In a short distance, a hawk cries out as it perched it-self high on the roof of an old house, while its wood shingles laid scattered about as if hit by a great wind. Pushing his way through a shield of small trees and bushes. he stands back in disbelief as the house was almost buried behind a grove of trees. While the thick vines seem to stretch its arms as if embracing the house in a way of protection. The unkempt yard and grey timber only added to the unsettling feeling he felt in the pit of his stomach. Again, he questions why he even came out this far. Ross lightly taps on the front door as uncertainty tells him to pick up the walking stick that was lying next to the house. He pulls from his thoughts as he rattles the latch. It was here amongst the thick dust and cob-webs he sees a distorted face looking back at him through the small window of the door. And for a long moment, he stared into the faded green eyes of the kontiksten'okonha (old woman).

Slowly the door opens, what stood before him ran a chill up his back. Her crooked back and tangled grey hair only added to why he should turn and run. For an endless time he couldn't grasp what he was looking at, her green eyes seemed to have changed. He could of sworn for just a moment one eye was yellow. He smiles an uneven smile as he realized the things he had seen along the path began to make sense. The dark haired woman he had seen at the fork of the road and the cries of the yellow eye hawk that led the way. She knew exactly who was coming along the path. She could shape shift.

At that moment the old woman reached out clutching his wrist as she guided him to a table. "You must drink the cup of tea set out for you, the leaves will tell what lies ahead," she said.

Ross thought it was odd that dust and leaves seem to be on everything, yet the steaming yohon:ronteh (tea kettle) sat noticeably clean, except for a small patch of black soot that sat long the bottom. Satken'se ne kanerahta o:kon (The leaves will tell what lies ahead). Again he questions his thoughts as an unnerving feeling began to fill around him; after all he hadn't seen any smoke coming from the chimney when he arrived. He nervously brushes the leaves from his seat as he reminds himself why he was here and quickly takes a sip of tea.

She spoke of an old man that crossed his yard near dusk. "You have seen him. His thoughts are unsettled," the seer said. "He wants something from you."

Ross admits he knew the man she was describing, but he had since passed away. He tells the old woman that after his uncle's death, he would wake in the middle of the night having a strange feeling of a hand lightly brushing the length of his face. He had dismissed the odd feeling, thinking he must have been waking from a dream. Still at times he would complain to his wife that he felt someone was sitting at the end of the bed.

The seer urged Ross to prepare for a feast to help the spirit to pass. But first the man's family must gather his clothes and what he held dear to him, material things, even things he had found in his travels, and give them away, she scolded.

Ross came home with an armful of things after the feast, his uncle's favourite sweater, a book, a metal medallion, and an old picture and frame that held a youthful time of his uncle. Ross put the small things in a wooden box and hung his uncle's favourite picture on the wall. Lastly, he smiled a satisfying smile as he carried in an old wooden rocking chair and sat it in living room.

Ross was a retired carpenter, if that was possible. There was hardly a day that went by that his wife wouldn't see him loading some of his tools into the back of that old truck.

"They just need help. Enkheyenawahse (I will help them). It won't take long," Ross said.

Ross had a good heart, but the long days were wearing him down, especially with the heatwave that didn't seem to be going away that summer. After cooking up a few venison steaks on his homemade grill that day, he stood back and smiled. A few large rocks and the metal shelf he had saved from a kaka:yen yekhonnya'táhkwa'(old cook stove), he smiled again as he remembered. It didn't cost him anything.

Halfway through cleaning the grill, he sat the brush down. Ross's steps were slow as he crossed the lawn. His lower back felt heavy as he pulled himself up onto the back steps. A sigh escaped from his mouth as his hand felt the handrail wobble beneath him. It was much too hot, he told his wife. The grill will have to wait till morning. He immediately suggested to his wife that he would sleep on the cot in the living room that night. Their two children were now fast asleep in their beds while a slight breeze fell over them from the only screen window.

"It will be a good time to read my uncle's book," he suggested to his wife as she handed him niwahsira'ah (a small blanket).

He latched the screen door and checked where he had kicked off his shoes earlier. A routine check he made every night. A warm smile spread across his face when he found a tall jar with his favourite strawberry drink sitting along the edge of the small table. His thoughts raced back to a few days before when he came home exhausted from a long day. His wife never acknowledged he was even home that day. He wondered then if she even cared.

Stretching out on the cot and for that instant he felt a faint breeze coming through the screen door. His eyes slightly closed for a moment as he remembered tomorrow was his day to rest. Suddenly he could hear movement along the wooden steps just outside the screen door. Thinking it was just a stray dog walking through his yard, he continued to read his book.

It was in these seconds that he heard the screen door slowly open. Ross turned just in time to see what he believed was a fragment form of a man standing just inside the doorway, although it was only for a moment. Slowly he could hear the sounds of the floorboards creaking as if someone was crossing the floor just in front of him.

Who or whatever it was had stopped just in front of his newly acquired rocking chair. The chair began to slowly rock for a frightening ten minutes. It was here in that instant he could see the image of an old man rise up, his shoulders bowed, his head lowered. Again he listens, as he can hear that faint sound of someone stepping along the floorboard. Slowly the screen door opened and in that moment he hears himself exhale as the door shut.

The next day he never said a word to his family, but returned the rocking chair.

Beth Returns Home

The stories had now come to an end and for a long moment I stared into the fire pit as the last ember faded into the darkness. Onen ki wahi (Goodbye then) I heard several say. I couldn't help but feel a loss as I wiped a tear from my eye. I had met so many people. The stories brought me a little closer to this land and to understanding of their beliefs. Lastly, I found a connection with the Jacket Hill family.

The long twisted trail back uphill seemed longer than I expected with the low batteries of my flashlight. And for a moment I turned back, I could almost hear the drums beating a familiar sound while their wailing voices continued filling my heart and soul.

"It's not much longer and you can sleep on the way home," I told my sons encouraging them to hurry, as most of the people were gone. At the top of the hill against the shadows of the trees sat an elderly woman on a tree stump, her hand immediately reached out as I was about to step pass. "My name is Grace, younger sister to Charlie. Your mother Cora was good friend of mine."

I smiled as I nervously took the thin notebook she was handing me. "My information is all in there and hope we can meet in a few days to exchange our stories." Grace's grandson then stepped forward guiding her along the path as Beth and her sons stood in disbelief.

In the days that followed, Beth would learn she had many relatives within the Hill (Jacket) side of the family.

When we arrived at the car, Emily and Silas along with her two brothers Carter and Gil were waiting. I smiled as I looked round to say goodbye to Isaac. Silas broke into laughter.

"Ráonha wahahtén:ti orhenkéhtsih (He did leave early). Maybe you will see him along the way," Silas said with a silly grin.

I think my children fell asleep by the time I turned onto the main road. I hadn't driven more than a couple miles when I began to see a ball of light weaving in and out between the trees. Then, just as I turned with the bend of the road that strange ball of light began to dart in front of the car, back and forth as if playing a game. When I looked back in the rear view mirror for a moment, I could have sworn it was Isaac standing along the side of the road his arm stretched high as he waved goodbye. In that instant, an old memory came to mind of seeing Isaac removing the dehydrated corn from his rooftop.

"It will make kanòntari:yo (a good soup) ne onen enyo'keren:onh (when the snow flies)," he had said.

Acknowledgements

Thank you to Virve Wiland and to my sisters Roberta Hill and Dawn Hill for reading countless drafts of my book and providing valuable comments.

Special thanks to Roger Milton Hill (Rakwatakwas) for bringing my stories to life with his knowledge of the Mohawk language. After long hours of roofing all day, he took the time to stop by after work to help me add the Mohawk language to my story. When I asked Roger how much should I pay him for his help, he replied, "Just make me a bologna sandwich every once in while."